ANN DENTON
KATIE MAY

LE RUE PUBLISHING

Le Rue Publishing

Cover by Carol Marques Designs

978-1-951714-14-7

To all of you with a Christmas wish, we hope it comes true. Unless you're wishing for more of 2020. If that's the case, get fucked.

PROLOGUE

CALVUS

WHY DID I think we could do this?

Break into the North Pole of all places, one of the most protected communities in all of angel history? Why did I let them talk me into this?

Why? Why? Why?

I run a hand through my sandy-blond hair as I stand with my brothers at the very top of a large snowy hill. There appears to be a small town down below us, tiny houses with mushroom roofs poking through the skeletal tree branches blanketed with snow. Eight-foot tall candy canes designed as streetlamps dot the road. Red and green pathways, each one lit up with multi-colored Christmas lights strung on picket fences that peek out of the snow drifts. And finally, in the distance, a warehouse hewn of dark wood with a shiny red roof —Santa's Workshop.

"If we do this, we'll go down in history," Demosthenes —Dem—says, rubbing his hands together with an eager glint in his eyes. He's always been the most daring member of our demon murder. He thrives off the thrill, the chase, the hunt. It's what makes him an excellent pickpocket and thief in Hell. Back when he was alive, centuries ago, he was considered one of the greatest thieves to ever live... Of course, he died shortly after they said that, the irony. Gunshot wound to the chest, because the dumbass got caught stealing from some noble lady after he fucked her.

And now, he's enjoying Hell with the best of us.

He's part of our murder, a group of demons banded together for strength in the endless fight against Heaven's puritanical bullshit.

"It's too cold," Brynjarr whines, already sagging heavily against a glaring Zorgos. Zorgos—or Gus, as we call him—immediately shoves the sloth demon to the ground, his lips quirking in a semblance of a smile when Bryn's immediately submerged in six feet of snow. "Fuck you." Bryn's voice is muffled, and I half wonder if he's already asleep. That's confirmed only a moment later when a loud snore erupts from the demon-shaped hole in the snow. Sloth demons.

2

They can hardly stay awake long enough to insult you.

Gus just grins, his tongue tapping his lip ring as his eyes focus on our target. "Let's fuck shit up." He cracks his tattooed neck and pumps his black wings once. As a wrath demon, he's always itching for a fight.

"I got 'em." Nicomedes strolls forward with a cocky-ass grin, and I just barely contain my groan. As a frustration demon, Nico thrives on this shit—pissing every living thing the fuck off. And non-living things. I'm pretty sure he made a cup irritated once on a dare.

He was drunk. I was drunk. Don't ask.

His fiery red hair flames around his face as he kneels beside the hole, his fucking red and green kilt pulling up to give me an unwanted view of his ass and the tip of his dick.

Motherfucker.

Before any of us can stop him, Nico jumps into the hole, balls first, and lands on Bryn's face with a "Whoop!" Of course, his battle cry wakes Bryn up instantly...or it could be the hairy ballsack millimeters from the sloth demon's mouth.

"Fer Scotland!" Nico cries, still attached to his homeland centuries after death and moving through the demon ranks.

"You fucker!" Bryn shouts as he gets tea-bagged.

As the two of them begin to tussle in the snow, disturbing the landscape and causing flurries to waft across my face, I turn towards Gus, who's, unsurprisingly, still scowling. Wrath demons don't often smile.

"We need a plan." I use the pad of my middle finger to push my glasses back into place. As a demon, I don't actually need glasses, but it's a habit I've had since I was human. At least, I assume it was. Unlike Dem, who has brief flashes of being a world-renowned thief, I don't have any memories of my human life. I just know that I have a desperate craving for chocolate twenty-four seven, I love my women kinky, and I like fiddling with my glasses.

"Easy!" Dem slings his arms over the two of us, a wide, shit-eating grin on his pretty boy face. "You go in," he nods at me, "and talk Santa into giving us his kingdom with that silver tongue of yours."

Ah. Yes. My power…or sin, as the case may be. White lies. It's how I deceived my way up the ladder in Hell and became a powerful leader, one of the few murder teams that no one can go up against. Maybe Raz—the devil's right-hand man—and his team could take us, but they've been a bit preoccupied lately on Earth.

"And if that doesn't work?" Gus demands, hurling daggers with his eyes at an unrepentant Dem.

"Then I'll steal it," Dem answers smugly, holding out his hand and showing me my fucking watch. When did he take it from my wrist?!?

This is why I shouldn't have allowed a kleptomaniac on my team. I resist the urge to swipe it back from him.

"We need an actual plan," I insist, gazing far out onto the horizon. Demons everywhere are desperate to claim the North Pole as their own. To take down Santa and his army of cherubs in the Christmas realm. And if my murder were to get it...

I can already imagine the celebration waiting for us back in Hell. The food, the wine, the sexy female demons using their forked tongues to suck on my horns.

But that isn't the only reason why I brought my team here. There's another one...a silver cord propelling me forward and reaching towards—

I shake my head vehemently to clear the thought.

"You looked at the blueprints dozens of times. You canna tell me you're second-guessing now," Nico says as he and Bryn move to join us, both completely covered in a fine layer of snow. Nico turns towards me, his face red from the cold, and continues, "We stop at Santa's house first. That'll be a good craic, incapacitating the big man. Then move on to his workshop.

The dafty cherubs in town will fall in line. Easy peasy, lemon squeezy, eh?"

"Until another demon group comes and tries to take the North Pole from us," Gus grumbles, always a downer. Seriously, if Gus were born human, instead of being made by the devil herself, he would be the type that would wear all black and sit in a dark room and brood. Tattoos, piercings, jars of blood… He's *that* type of broody. Actually, he has all those things already.

"Don't be a fookin' wank stain," Nico says, always stirring shit up. Gus's eyes flare brightly in challenge, looking seconds away from strangling the frustration demon.

"Enough!" I move to step between them and release a heavy sigh. I swear I feel a migraine coming on, which is ridiculous, because demons can't get headaches. But those two… "We need to move in the cover of night. Is everybody ready?"

And that…

That, my friends, is when everything goes to *shit*.

Before any of them can respond, the ground beneath us begins to shake, almost as if an earthquake is rippling through the ground. Bryn doesn't even bother to try and stay upright, immediately falling to his ass with a bored expression on his face. Nico grins as if this is all a big game, while Gus's scowl deepens. Only Dem seems to understand the urgency of the situation as he glances at me, his black wings unfurling from his back. They stretch wide, the razor-sharp talons at the top looking especially menacing and deadly.

"What the fuck?" His eyes narrow at the figure approaching from the town, moving at a pace that I would almost describe as indolent. Bored. As if we're beneath his notice and not a threat in the slightest.

I take a moment to see a muscular older gentleman dressed in a red, crisp suit with a pressed shirt and gold cufflinks. His white hair is artfully styled away from his arresting face and proud cheekbones, and his beard has been trimmed delicately. He swings around a cane as if he has all the fucking time in the world. As if he's just taking a leisurely stroll down Candy Cane Road. I'm not into dudes at all, but he's a serious DILF.

"Motherfooker…" Nico breathes, his accent kicking up a notch in fear.

"Watch your tone, boy," the man says snidely, a mischievous twinkle in his jolly eyes. "Or else I'll put you on the naughty list."

Motherfucker is right.

Santa.

Holy crap. One of the most powerful of all of the archangels. He's built an entire empire for God and goodness and walking the disgustingly straight and narrow path. My mouth dries out as I see him up close for the first time.

"But," Santa continues as my wings extend from my back and my claws lengthen, "it appears you've already been bad boys." He holds his cane up, and at the top, I can see what looks like a snow globe. Only instead of artificial snow and a pretty display, there's what appears to be a ball of magic. Bright red sparks interspersed with mossy green—Santa's magical signature.

He's still fucking beaming a smile at us, as if this is the most exciting thing that has ever happened to him. Hell, maybe it is.

But I don't get a chance to fight back, to defend my murder, when he aims the cane in our direction…

And all Hell breaks loose.

1

JOY

OUTSIDE, it's a balmy negative two degrees. In the lane, snow is glistening under the moon's soft light, and I can hear the jingle of bells as some of the reindeer take the sleigh out for a nighttime test drive. I should be at home in the kitchen, humming and pulling a fresh sheet of gingerbread cookies—Mom's recipe—out of the oven to cool and fill the house with Christmas scents. But I'm not.

I'm out on a date with a guy I met in Christmas Village. Or maybe I should say, I'm currently attempting to escape from said date via the ladies' bathroom window. But The Drunken Elf didn't properly plan for women's needs. This window is way too damn high!

Don't they realize that women need to sneak away from gropey dates? Especially ones who've admitted they've really taken to their latest hobby—creating Victorian hair wreaths. Yes, wreaths made of hair. Human hair.

I shudder, remembering how Alan reached towards me, his green wings trembling in delight. The dragon shifter had leaned forward, his ruffled white shirt collar nearly dragging through his lamb soup—he had a very steampunk look—as he fingered one of my long blonde locks, a strange longing in his eyes that I don't think had anything to do with sex.

Thank goodness. But also not. Not goodness. Because hair wreaths are up there with skin suits in the icky department.

My horror movie fetish surfaces and makes drunken me shudder, thinking about Buffalo Bill and Hannibal Lector. This is a *very bad thing*, since I currently have one shoeless foot propped up on the bathroom sink and the other lifted in midair, attempting to gain purchase on the window ledge. It's not a good position for shuddering. Or much of anything.

My groin whines in protest as I try and stretch just a bit further.

"Cupid's left nut! This is hard!" I huff as my foot swipes futilely at the ledge.

Nope.

It's not gonna happen. I give one last longing look at my escape hatch before carefully climbing down and sliding back into my white, fur-lined high-heeled boots. I untuck my green and red paneled skirt from my pantyhose and straighten the off-the-shoulder fur collar. The festive wreath in my hair somehow survived my climb, so I don't fix it. I just stare into the mirror and make a disgusted face at myself. "Why couldn't you inherit the wings?" I ask my reflection.

She doesn't have answers, not any more than Dad does. Sometimes half-angel children get the wings, sometimes they don't. Unfortunately, it appears Santa's daughter isn't cool enough to fly like the big angels. No wings for me. Which means no escaping from shitty dates. I'm just going to have to face the music. I'll have to march back out there to Alan and…

Lie.

My mother, Ali, was human. As a half-human, that means I can lie. In a village full of angels…it's quite the perk.

Yes. Christmas is run by angels. Not elves. Duh. Did you really think elves would be so selfless? Not by a longshot.

I blow out a big breath and shake out my hands, just as a cherub with Dolly Parton hair enters the bathroom.

"Oh hey, Joy!" she calls.

"Hey!" I give her a wave and a smile.

"Having a nightcap after a long day at the workshop," she tells me, adjusting her white sweater as she walks towards a stall. "You?"

"Same." See? Lying is beneficial. Now all the cherubs at the office will not know about this humiliating attempt to get myself laid. And if they don't know, that means news won't get back to my father. You know, the big guy. The person who puts jolly in…well, jolly.

"Well, see you tomorrow! Hope you're making some of those reindeer sugar cookies for the breakroom!"

"I'll add it to my baking list," I say through gritted teeth and a fake ass smile. I hate when the cherubs put in orders, which they do all the time! It stifles my creativity. Just let me bake! Grr.

That little pet peeve rubs my insides like one-hundred grit sandpaper.

Yes, Santa's daughter knows her sandpapers, all right? Comes with the territory.

I make my way back over to the table, where I find Alan using a knife to slice off a bit of the waitress's hair. Not even scissors. He's using his steak knife, and she's letting him because angels can be so utterly stupid sometimes. How motherfucking creepy is that?

Okay, Michael Meyers, now I'm not even faking stomach cramps for your benefit. I decide just to ghost him. I slide sideways along the back wall of the bar towards the coat closet.

I hiss at Larry, the cherub manning the coats. "I need my cloak please."

It feels like an eternity while he digs around in the back, fluttering from coat to coat and checking a million tags. My eyes flicker impatiently between him and my date at the table.

When I notice Alan stand up at the table, gazing around the bar, I literally dive into the coat closet.

"Whoa! What happened?" Larry asks in concern.

"I fell," I lie, reaching up and snagging my white cloak, which is nearly impossible to spot if you don't know what you're looking for. Angels wear almost exclusively white, but I had a red lining put on mine after I'd lost my fifth cloak in one year. Now, the angels won't touch it. Bonus, the lining is velvety soft.

Larry mutters concerned phrases like "Oh dear, are you all right?" and other generic nonsense that I ignore.

I throw on my cloak and pull up my hood, then peer carefully around the edge of the doorjamb.

Alan's back is to me, green wings tucked in.

Score!

I bolt for the door and don't even care when I'm blasted by arctic wind as I step out into the night. Instead, I tilt my face up and admire the aurora borealis that stretches between the human realm and ours for a second before hurrying across the street through the snow. Luckily, the sleighs packed it down today, but there are still drifts as tall as houses in places. No one ever wanders off the road in Christmas Village. They stick to the straight and narrow path.

But of course they do. They're angels.

I open the door to the stable, which is packed tonight. Cheery golden lanterns hanging from the ceiling give the barn a golden glow. Unfortunately, the smell of the place is not nearly as good as the look of it. Every stall is full, and some reindeer are even squished in two to a stall. I guess everyone and their brother has ridden their reindeer out to the town.

It is getting close to Christmas, so it makes sense that they all want to decompress before the twenty-four-hour shifts start.

"Blitzen!" I call out, trying not to step too far into the hay-strewn barn. Parking stables are not very hygienic places.

A low groan sounds, and a massive reindeer emerges from one of the stalls, hay sticking out of either side of his mouth. "You goofy boy! Have you been eating this whole time?" My voice automatically reverts to a baby tone, and the smile on my face is automatic.

I love the reindeer. They're one of my favorite things about the North Pole.

Blitzen trots over, opening his mouth and just letting bits of hay drop off his tongue. I laugh. "You're so lazy! Come on, I'm ready to go home!"

At the word "home," his brown ears perk up and his eyes widen. He walks a bit faster, butting my shoulder with his head in what I deem a reindeer hug. When we get just outside the stable door, I shove it closed, and then Blitzen pauses near a stump. I climb up onto the stump and then use it to help me mount his back.

Once my legs are on, he jolts forward. I hurry to grab onto his antlers so that I don't fall off. "Whoa, big boy! What's your hurry?"

Blitzen moans out something that I'm certain is a reply in reindeer-speak. Unfortunately, I have no idea what it means.

I move my hands, trying to slide them down from his horns so that I can find the reins, but as soon as I do, he moves from a walk into a jolting trot, and I have to grab back on to his horns and squeeze for dear life.

"Blitz! Are you crazy?" I squeal as he picks up speed and darts down the road, rounding a corner.

Of course, there's a reason I picked Blitzen. Out of all the reindeer, he's the absolute laziest. His little jaunt doesn't last longer than sixty seconds before he slows back down to a walk. Sixty more seconds, and his pace is absolutely glacial. I chose him tonight because he typically has the perfect pace for a drunken ride home, or a drunken ride of shame home the next morning.

The wind picks up, and magical little snowflakes dance around us as Blitz leads me back towards my little log cabin.

To my amusement, but not surprise, Blitzen's favorite pals are waiting for us. Grouped around my front door are Cupid, Comet, Donner, and Dasher. The five reindeer are like a little club, always hanging out together. And for some reason, they've adopted me, which really seems to irk Dad.

But I've got a way with animals, what can I say?

They love my cookies. And the belly rubs I give them, though I constantly have to tell Comet to stop getting a red rocket when I scratch his belly. And they really, *really* love it when I stroke their horns. I didn't think animal horns were that sensitive, but I guess that just shows how little I know.

"My guys." I smile when I see them, my heart warming. They're so loyal. And they would *never* make a wreath out of my hair.

A chorus of lows and bellows reaches my ears as they say hello back to me. Cupid sits calmly back, watching the others come to greet me, while Comet runs around me in circles, his teeth nipping at the pair of gloves in my back pocket, the scoundrel. Donner rolls onto his belly, demanding tummy rubs, while Dasher gives him the reindeer equivalent of a scowl and annoyed huff.

"Gosh, I just love you guys," I say. "I had the worst date in the history of the world! Who wants to hear about it while I bake cookies?"

More lows and bellows.

I giggle. "All right then. Come on. Let's go to the workshop kitchen, because there's no way all five of you will fit into my tiny cabin. And if you need to do your business…do it now. Anyone who makes a mess on the floor there will not get any of my cookies!"

Five reindeers immediately poop, including the one I'm riding.

I laugh uproariously. I really didn't expect them to understand me at all. But just like the horn thing, I make all kinds of assumptions about animals. I really should do some research on them, but I'm not much of a book person. Unless it's a recipe book.

We head down to Santa's Workshop, a massive facility made out of trees that are as big around as some of the redwoods in California. A red metallic roof can hardly be seen under the snow that covers it like a blanket.

Even though it's the middle of the night, there are still lights on inside the toy-making side of the building, because the angels take spreading Christmas cheer seriously, and there are twenty-four-seven shifts. I don't go over there, because I selfishly don't want to get caught up in helping to meet quotas.

I open the side door that leads to the massive kitchen I inherited from Mom and hold it open for the reindeer.

No, it wasn't locked. Angels don't do locks. No need.

Once all my boys are in, I flip on the lights and look around at my kitchen. My cabinets are all painted a bright cheery green. I have pristine white countertops. And all of my appliances are cherry red. I give a sigh of pure relaxation. This kitchen is my happy spot. My retreat.

"Okay, now, let's vote on cookies!" I tell the guys.

Donner bucks up onto his hind legs, pawing the air with excitement. Of course, he accidentally kicks Dasher in the face, and I swear the other reindeer looks seconds away from murdering him and then creating a coat out of his fur.

"All right, boys, you remember the rules. One tap only. You can only vote for one type of cookie. Got it?" I narrow my eyes and focus in on Cupid. He always double taps. Without fail. He stares back innocently, widening his big buck eyes at me.

I slide my gaze sideways to Comet, the reindeer with a white slash across his forehead that looks like a falling star. "You better not steal extra cookies, because some are going to be for Blitz." He's not great at sharing.

"And you, mister." I wag a finger at Donner, who's got the darkest eyes and markings of the bunch. "No trying to sneak pepper into my cookies this time."

Donner snorts in what I assume is laughter. He's a bit of a brat. He's always tripping the others and always trying to mess with my recipes. But still, he's so light-hearted and silly, his tongue lolling out of his face half the time, and I don't have the heart to do more than chastise him.

Fine. I spanked him once. But he kept backing his ass into my hand after that, so I think he misinterpreted it as some kind of weird butt scratch. So I don't do it anymore.

Blitzen, worn out from having to actually walk, sinks to his knees in the corner and then onto his side. He splays out on the black and white-tiled floor.

"Settling in for your long winter nap?" I quip.

Blitzen's hoof clops against the tiles once.

"Want me to wake you up for cookies?" I ask.

Another clop.

"All right. Go to sleep, sweetie, and thanks for the ride home." I wink at him, and I swear it looks like he tries to wink back. Or maybe that's just what a reindeer who's about to pass out does. Like I said, I don't research these things.

I turn to the four remaining reindeer, and Donner leans forward to nip my ear gently. Not biting down, just grazing my skin with his giant teeth.

"Whoa, boy," I laugh. "Okay! Okay, we'll vote." I shove his big furry head away and say, "Line up so I can make sure there is no cheating."

The four reindeer line up like good little soldiers, their massive chests at the same height as my face.

"All right, if you want biscochitos, the anise cookies, stomp once."

Cupid stomps.

"If you want traditional sugar cookies, stomp once." Comet stomps, and Cupid stomps again.

I wag a finger at Cupid. "That doesn't count."

He wrinkles his nose.

"Gingerbread men," I say. Dasher and Donner both clop.

"All right! We have a winner!" I declare. "And since none of you can talk, I get to pick the music!" I flip on the CD player, an old school device we have to have up here because there's no radio signal. I press play, but "Santa Baby" comes on, and I immediately recoil.

There are just some things you don't want to imagine your Dad doing, and slipping things under other women's *trees* is one of them.

I press the button to skip to the next track. "Rudolph, the Red-Nosed Reindeer" starts up, and the reindeer all groan, but I laugh and leave it, because a little humility is good for them, right? Besides, the truth is Rudolph's actually a female who tried…err…mating with every single one of them. It did not end well. Dad had to transfer the horny bitch to a separate division, and I'm pretty sure my reindeer are traumatized to this day.

I hum along as I open up my cupboards, grabbing things that we'll need. Donner follows along behind me and takes the items one by one with his mouth as I hand them to him, but when I'm all done and I turn towards my big island so we can get mixing, I don't see anything.

Not my mixer. Not my spices. Not my rolling pin.

I whirl and glare at Comet, who's been known to steal my socks.

I've found them in his stall before, all crusty and gross with who-knows-what.

"Comet!" I scold.

But that's when Donner starts snorting so hard, he wheezes.

I turn to face the bratty reindeer, tossing my hands onto my hips. "Are you stirring up trouble? You naughty reindeer. You just tried to frame your brother!" I dart forward and scratch him between the ears, reverting to baby talk again. "You're just the worstest. That's so meanie weanie of you."

He doesn't seem too repentant, because he keeps laughing.

Finally, I sigh and step back. "I'm going to go wash my hands. And when I turn back around, I expect all of my things to be on the island. Or no cookies." I bop his nose and then head to the sink.

When I turn back, everything is there, just like magic.

I smile wide and grin. "Okay, boys. Let's whip up some Christmas spirit."

And my night goes from awful to awesome, morphing from blech to delicious, just like the sugar and spice I stir together.

I sigh when I realize that Kristoff from *Frozen* had it right. "Reindeer are better than people." That's not a good sign for a girl on the dating market.

2

NICO, AKA DONNER

BEING TRAPPED in a reindeer body sucks ass. Do you ken how hard it is to prank someone when you're a fooking animal?

I've tried shitting in Santa's boots, chewing on the cherub's hair, tilting the sleigh upside down mid-flight. You know what happens, eh? People just sigh and shake their heads or pat my head like I'm special.

It leaves me scunnered and sad.

There is nothing worse for a frustration demon than the inability to annoy the shit out of people. Ugh. I wish I could chew gum, my nervous habit from back when I had a normal body, before Santa turned our murder of demons into reindeer with that magical cane of his.

I used to hate him for it and plan my revenge on the stupid stoter, but at the end of the day, after a decade of answering to "Donner," the memories of being a demon have faded a bit. Not the urges. I still really want to scuttle plans and hear those amazing screams of frustration. And I still want to rut…I mean fook…women.

My lids lower and my eyes grow sultry when I watch one lass in particular approach the barn this afternoon. Joy. Santa's daughter has perfect wide hips, the type I'd love to see spread beneath me as I fook her in my stall…I mean a bed. A bed.

See what a decade as a hoofed animal does? Even my fantasies have been affected. I canna think a dirty thought straight through without having the reindeer shit affect it. I sigh, not bothering to correct the strange turns my thoughts take as I envision a naked Joy sprawled out in the hayloft, me thrusting into her and leaning forward to snag a bit of hay for a snack at the same time.

"Dude, stop giving Joy your 'fuck me' eyes." Gus—aka Dasher—bumps me with his shoulder. Stupid wrath demon is always trying to start shit, even as a damn deer. The angels probably only hear a strange, braying sound, but fook them. It's their fault we're in this mess.

"Shut it," I tell him. "'Fook me' eyes are all I got these days."

"I wonder if she's brought us more cookies," Cupid— aka Cal, our leader—asks. "I could really use a chocolate hit right now." He's obsessed with her chocolate chip cookies.

"You sure that's the cookie you're thinkin' aboot?" I ask, smiling as Cal's black reindeer lips thin.

"Keep your mind out of the gutter," he quips. "Of course I'm not thinking about that." Cal is a liar, so I don't believe him at all, but I'm happy to have frustrated him a little by calling him out.

We're all tied to a long post outside the stable, waiting for some cherubs to come hook us up to the sleigh for a practice run. It's been snowing all day, and those dumb fooks keep going inside to warm up, leaving our furry asses in the cold. I swear, they inhale cocoa like it's cocaine. They take hot chocolate breaks more times per day than a Kardashian takes duck-lipped selfies. No wonder they're fat. Stupid halo humpers.

Would it annoy them if I subscribed them all to some weight loss magazines? I'm not sure that I could get delivery from the human realm, but the urge to try fills me like an itch, traveling all the way from my nose to my toes. But I canna scratch it, because I don't have fingers. Hooves are the pits.

Now that I ken that, I'll totally have more pity for the demons back home who've been born with cloven hooves. Opposable thumbs are really a masterpiece.

A chubby cherub wanders out of the barn to our post, his rotund tummy peeking out underneath his turtle-neck, because nobody told him that those things all got burned on Earth at the end of the eighties for being fooking lame. The Christmas realm is stuck in a bit of a time warp.

My eyes are drawn away from Joy, who is approaching from down the road, her gorgeous blonde locks billowing in the bit of wind. Instead, my gaze lands on that tempting tummy, which is getting closer and closer.

I love nipping cherubs' little tummy rolls whenever I can reach them. Unfortunately, most of them can see me coming because reindeer horns are *goddamned fooking heavy*. There is no quick turn of the head or sleight of anything with thirty-three pounds of hard bone stacked on top of your skull.

Next to me, Calvus sighs dreamily. I turn back to see him staring at Joy with the world's dopiest expression. I might give her "fook me" eyes, but Santa was right to name him Cupid. The fool's been a lovesick mess since the day he saw her. And he won't say why.

I glance back over at her. I mean, she *is* quite bonnie. She's a willowy blonde with legs for days. I love watching her mount my brothers because her skirts get pulled back and I get to glimpse those delicious thighs…

And she has a laugh that's more delicate than silver bells.

She actually likes reindeer, which none of the cherubs assigned to the stables do. They're all just waiting to get called up to the big leagues—Santa's Workshop.

Joy grows closer, and the scent of sugar cookies wafts over, as if the sweetness is embedded in her very skin. It very nearly is. I've licked her a few times to check. I canna resist it.

I run my tongue over my lips, swiping some of my fur in the wrong direction—add it to the list of annoyances. You're keeping a list right? And checking it twice?—but I can barely focus on the feel of hair that's parted the wrong way.

Because Joy smiles.

And something inside of my chest lights up like a star on top of a Christmas tree.

I find my expression relaxing into the same dopey grin that I just mocked Cal for.

Joy asks us, "How are my sweet boys today?" She uses baby talk, and I dinnae even mind. She turns to the cherub, and her voice takes on a serious tone. "Hey, Blizzard, do you think I could steal these guys away for a second?"

Blizzard glances at his watch. "No can do. Test flight starts in ten."

"Oh, but I just saw a sleigh down in the village that crashed into a snowbank!" she exclaims, letting her luminous green eyes grow wide. "I was hoping these reindeer could help pull it out!"

Blizzard's jaw drops in alarm. "Oh! Oh! Of course, Ms. Kringle. Go right ahead." He flutters his wings and flies over to the wooden post and starts untying us. "Do you need my help? They're a lot to manage, especially this one!" He bops my nose reprovingly when my teeth get too close to his stomach.

"Oh no, thank you. I brought some cookies to reward them." Joy's smile turns up a few watts, and I get an inkling that makes my hooves start to prance around.

That smile looks fake. It looks…naughty. I canna resist a naughty Joy.

Next to me, Cal says, "Fuck yes, lie to him, baby." As a white lie demon, nothing gets him revved up more than watching a girl lie to someone else. Of course, since he's stuck in a reindeer body, all that Joy and the cherub hear is a low moan.

"Don't worry, Cupid." Joy reaches up and strokes Cal's neck. "Your friends will help. I'll strap you all up, and you can all work together."

"Did that sound dirty to anyone else?" Demosthenes asks, momentarily distracted from his attempt to nip the keys that are in the cherub's pocket. Even our thievery demon is distracted from his stealing by her.

"She can strap me up any time. I love sex swings," Brynjarr responds, pushing off the post and trotting forward to sniff her pockets. "Yes. There are at least eight cookies in there. I call dibs on first pick!" he declares before he yawns. I doubt he'll be awake long enough to call dibs. That sloth demon is the laziest fook I know.

"Come on, boys!" Joy calls out, oblivious to the red rocket I end up sporting when I peek down the front of her dress.

"Do you need some rope?" the dopey cherub asks, hovering way too close to me.

"Oh no, they already have some. I just need some muscle." She winks at him and grabs my lead, tugging me towards the road. The other guys follow, and I let my eyes enjoy the view of her ass as we tromp down the street.

One day, we're going to be ourselves again. One day, I'm gonna walk up to Joy and just grab her, swing her into my arms, and dip her. Then I'm going to ravage her mouth with kisses until she begs me to ravish other parts of her.

Until that day, I'll happily follow along with whatever silly scheme she's got.

We come to a curve in the road, passing some candy cane shaped light poles and entering a less populated part of Christmas Village, where the road isn't lined with gingerbread-looking houses but faced with evergreen trees. The trees block some of the wind from the blizzard, but not the cold. Snowflakes as big as my hooves tumble down from the sky, looking just as lacey as those that human children cut out of paper. Fookin' Christmas magic making it all enchanted looking.

Joy turns back to look at us, a wicked twinkle in her eye. "So, in case you hadn't realized, boys, there is no sleigh! I busted you out for a last day of freedom before the big countdown!"

Dasher—I mean Gus—bounds down the open road and leaps into the air, flying just because. Maybe he's working out some of his rage. It's something Santa never lets us do, like he's afraid we'd fly off and leave his ass. Maybe we would. But we wouldna do that to Joy.

"So, who wants to give me a ride?"

"Oh, me!" Bryn perks up for once in his fooking life. "You can ride me any time, Christmas princess!" our sloth demon calls.

"Hell no, you got the last turn." Cal lowers his horns and rams Bryn, who barely lowers his own antlers in time to block the hit. The sloth demon is the worst at battle.

"Well, don't mind if I do." Dem runs around them and quickly kneels down so Joy can climb up onto his back, effectively stealing everyone else's shot, the arsehole.

"Thank you, Comet," she says, patting the white shooting star mark on his furry forehead. You can see his grin, even on his animal face.

"Fooking theivery demon," I call out. "Go bile yer hed!" My accent comes out so strong, I can't even say boil.

"Snooze and lose," he retorts, standing up carefully with Joy on his back. "Oh man, those thighs feel sooo good wrapped around me. Yeah, baby, scoot up. Make yourself comfy. Daddy's gonna take you for the ride of your life."

I blow a raspberry at him, which just makes Joy laugh.

"Oh, make her laugh some more. Wonder if she'll come if I make her ride rough!"

"Don't you talk about her like that, you asswipe!" Cal yells.

Here's the thing about Cal—he never yells. White lie demons love smoothing things over, lulling people into a false sense of security.

I turn to him and arch a brow. At least, I think I do. With stupid fooking animal features being as confusing as they are, I canna tell. "Whoa. What's up with you?"

"She's our…" Cal trails off, pawing at the ground.

He doesn't say it, but his silence slams into me with the force of a Mack truck.

"She's our what?" Bryn asks, his eyes drooping now that he's lost the chance of a "Joy-ride."

Cal swallows hard but meets my eyes like a man when he says, "She's our Center."

Ever had an inkling about something, like an intuitive gut feeling, eh? Well, having it confirmed is strange. It's an out-of-body experience. No, that's not right. I've had one of those, when I got turned into a damned animal. Hearing that Joy is our fated mate, our destiny, makes my body feel like it's floating through space.

I look down and realize that I'm floating somehow, hooves dangling above the ground. I must have activated the reindeer magic unconsciously.

My eyes travel over to Joy and Dem, who are diving down towards the snow-capped evergreens. Her hair is streaking out behind her, and she shrieks in delight, clutching Dem by the neck.

A feeling just rolls through me, like the crackle of a fire and the warm scent of cinnamon. It's like the featherlight white clouds that line the streets of Hell and tickle you when you walk barefoot. It's like the sight of mistletoe... A giant smile spreads inside of me.

Joy is *ours*.

I ken it. I mean, I didnae really, but then again, I did. Somehow, I knew.

Gus rises into the air and then swoops down and smashes into Cal, knocking him backwards into the snow. Cal quickly whips back onto his hooves, snorting his displeasure, which comes out as a puff of fog because the air is so fooking cold.

"What the fuck?" Cal asks.

"You knew! You knew she was our Center all these years and didn't tell us!" Gus is in full wrath demon mode. His reindeer eyes are even rimmed in red. Ohhh, he's more pissed than the men in a pub after a football match.

"What the hell were we supposed to do about it?" Cal rages back. "We're fucking deer!"

"I don't know! We could have—" He cuts off whatever he was about to say, which was probably violent. "We could have avoided her."

"You really want to avoid her?" Cal jerks his neck in the direction of Joy and Dem, who are now bounding up and down through the sky in a rainbow pattern. "She's the only good thing in this whole place—"

Gus shakes his head. "You just couldn't resist the fact that she lies, could you?"

Bryn sinks into the snow, tucking his legs underneath himself and getting comfortable as he watches the fight.

"Yeah, I like that she lies, okay? I admit it." Cal says.

"You're our fucking leader. You're supposed to warn us about Centers!" Gus snarls, baring his teeth.

"I'm supposed to warn you about dangers!" Cal retorts. "Joy *isn't* a danger!"

"Says the lying demon." Gus lifts off the ground with a swish and shoots back into the sky. I'm surprised he doesn't use those antlers and knock Cal in the chest with them.

My eyes travel back to Bryn, who's just tucked his head onto his knee and looks ready to pass out. Either this whole thing is so dramatic that he's overwhelmed, or he already guessed everything about Joy and isn't surprised at all. It's hard to ken with a sloth demon.

Cal sighs as he watches Gus bolt laps through the sky, ignoring the snowflakes that blow around him. "Think he'll forgive me?"

I shrug. "He's a wrath demon. He's basically wired to fly off the handle. I'm sure he'll calm down eventually."

I hear Joy call out, "Dasher! Oh boy, you're so fast! Come on down when you want cookies!"

Bryn perks up. "Did she say cookies?"

Joy and Comet—dammit, I mean Joy and *Dem* streak back down from the cloud-laden sky. Our gorgeous Center laughs when the shithead slides into his landing so he can spray us with snow like a right asshole.

And while Cal is distracted, that's when Gus decides to strike. He zooms over us and drops a deuce right onto Cal's head. I can't help but admire his aim.

"Ohhh! Cupid! Oh, I'm so sorry!" Joy's hand flies to her mouth as Cal dips his head forward and lets the steaming turd drop from his fur into the snow.

"Zorgos!" Cal bellows.

"Don't worry, buddy, we'll get you a bath. Come on. A nice warm bubbly bath will make you feel all better!"

Joy slides off of Dem's back and pulls out a corner of a cookie to tempt Cal.

"Bath? Joy's gonna give him a bath? Getting her clothes all wet…" Bryn immediately rolls into the shitpile.

"Blitzen, no!" she screeches, but it's too late. Bryn comes up with a brown stripe on his back that is not natural coloring.

Idiots. I'm in a murder full of fooking idiots.

Joy gathers up the reins for both of them. "You two are seriously out of control." She gives them a dark look, but it's undermined by the baby voice she uses for us. "Come on, you dopes."

Bryn looks back at me smugly. "I'm getting a bath! Our Center's hands are going to be all over me—"

Just then, we round the corner and find Blizzard, the cherub who'd been tending to the stables earlier. He's bundled up in a thick white snowsuit, only his balding blond head exposed.

"Joy! I was just looking for you! I didn't find a sleigh—"

"Oh, it was down this way." Joy gestures smoothly behind us. "Got it all worked out, but these two got into some stinky stuff."

Blizzard's nose crinkles as he gets a whiff. "Ugh. I can see that."

"So, if you could give them a bath, that'd be great!" She smiles brightly and forces the reins for Cal and Bryn into his hands before she turns towards me and Dem. "Come on, you two. You can help me bake the cookies while they get all clean."

I cannae help the way my shoulders shake with laughter at Bryn's heartbroken expression. I turn away and trot behind Joy without an ounce of regret, not even startled when Gus lands next to me and starts to walk alongside me. Apparently, even a right arsehole like himself can't stay away from our mate more than a few seconds. He can be pissed all he wants, but I see the way he looks at her. The way we *all* look at her.

The blizzard lets up, and a bit of sun peeks through. What more could a guy want? My soulmate's in front of me, ass swaying, we're on our way to make cookies…

Oh yeah…a body that's not *this fooking bullshit*. That's what more I could want.

3

JOY

I HUM ALONG to "The Little Drummer Boy" as I pull a sheet of fresh sugar cookies from the oven. They're golden brown on the edges, pale in the center, and they smell divine. I can't wait until we frost them. I set the cookies on the stovetop and shut the oven, then pull off one of my oven mitts in order to grab a spatula and transfer these little suckers to the cooling racks.

I grin when a loud smack sounds at the door of the workshop kitchen.

Behind me, Dasher groans. Aww, he's so excited that his friends are back! I hurry to the door and pull it open to reveal a freshly blow-dried Cupid and Blitzen. Blizzard even put little bows in their neck hair. How cute.

"Come on in, guys! I was just taking out a batch! Won't be long!"

Once they tromp inside, I shut the door and head back over to the stove.

BAAAM.

I duck behind the kitchen island as a huge sound rocks through the workshop, the percussive force causing a high-pitched ring to start up in my ears.

Oh no! Did the Christmas cracker machine explode again? We had that issue a few years back.

I stand and quickly check on my reindeer friends to see if they're ok. Blitzen is on the floor, blinking in surprise, half of his gingerbread reindeer still stuck out of the corner of his mouth.

Yes, they like to eat Christmas reindeer. The idea of pretend cannibalism amuses them endlessly. And I indulge them, because they're just silly animals and there's no harm in it.

I look over at Cupid, who's taken up a position in front of the rest of them. He's got a bit of a protective streak. His eyes narrow when he looks at me, as if he can predict what I'm about to say.

"You boys stay here. I'm gonna go see if the cherubs need any help."

Cupid very definitively shakes his head no. How adorable is that? He's just the sweetest. As I move around the kitchen towards the green interior door that leads to the workshop, I pat his neck.

"Don't worry, sweet boy, I'll be right back."

I pull open the door and go into the hallway. Cupid immediately follows, ducking his huge head so his antlers can fit through the door.

I turn around and stick my hands on my hips. "No, sir! You know reindeer aren't allowed in the workshop! Not since Blitzen tried to lay down with the teddy bears and popped the stitches on about eighty of them." I don't even bring up the fact that several hundred others had to be remade because the cherubs feared that kids would have allergy issues. "Turn right back around!" I order. But that's literally impossible because his horns are so wide that they barely fit through the doorway. There's no way he'll be able to turn around in this narrow hall.

I sigh. "Fine. You brat. Follow me. I'll have to let you out through one of the rolling doors where they make the Christmas cars for the Richie Rich kids."

Cupid trots behind me, getting so close that his head actually looms over mine and I can feel his hot breath on my neck.

His proximity should comfort me, but my instincts are screaming. My body is on high alert. For some reason, all the hairs on my arms stand up. Somehow, instinctively, I know something's wrong. Very wrong. I get a feeling that I've never had before. It's like an avalanche. Cold slides down my spine, and my stomach tumbles. I realize that I'm scared.

My hand flies to my heart as it starts beating more quickly in my chest, and I'm not quite sure what to do about it. I slide my feet forward despite my fear, because Dad always says, "A Kringle helps. That's what we were made to do."

I have to help the cherubs who were working in the workshop, the tiny little people who slave day in and day out to make the holiday memorable. Sometimes, they even don the silly elf outfits humans believe they wear, just for giggles.

I reach the end of the hall and find my palms are sweaty. There's a green door in front of me, with a little panel window above the knob. The word "Workshop" is scrolled in gold paint across the top. I grab the knob, but before I can turn it, a laugh echoes through the workshop.

It's not a happy laugh.

It's the kind of laugh I hear in my horror movies.

I freeze.

Through the little window, I see Dad. He's on the ground, his red suit wrinkled, his cane smashed against the ground, Christmas magic oozing across the floor like red and green blood.

NO!

I see Dad's wings erupt from his back, shredding the top of his suit, and he lifts up off the floor, his beard bedraggled but his eyes blazing. A white light starts to gather in his palms.

I didn't know Dad could do that!

But then a winged shadow appears behind him and slices at him with a sword.

Oh shit!

Dad swivels, his wings swishing in a move I've never seen before. He barrel rolls, the white light blasting at the shadow that I realize…has horns.

Dammit! It's a demon! We're being attacked by demons!

I turn sideways, glancing for the black metallic evil alarm box we had installed next to the red fire alarm, because these assholes try to take out Christmas every few years. I have to squish past Cupid to get to it. And that's when I realize that Cupid wasn't the only reindeer who followed me. All five of my reindeer have lined up in the hallway.

Another blast of sound comes from the workshop, and all of a sudden, I gag. My eyes water.

Oh hell!

One of the reindeers musked up the hall!

"Really?" I ask sarcastically, before realizing the shit scent is so strong that I can taste it. Whenever they're scared or territorial, deer shoot this nasty-ass—literally, it smells like ass—spray to deter others. It's really gaggingly effective. I shove a hand over my mouth as my eyes start to water, mentally blaming Blitzen and cursing his poor timing. I use the remaining hand to pull the evil alarm, and a trumpet-like blast sings out the first notes of "Oh Come All Ye Faithful" to warn the angels to come with weapons blazing.

It's only after I pull the alarm that I realize...my poor reindeer can't back up. We don't have a choice. We're going to have to join the fight.

As the only part-human in an all supernatural realm, that does not sound like a good idea. That sounds like bringing a knife to a gunfight.

But if we stay here, the reindeer are sitting ducks. They can't get out. And who would I be if I left them?

Dammit. I don't have a weapon. I turn and look at Cupid, lowering my hand from my nose so I can say, "We're gonna have to charge them. I don't know how many there are."

Cupid gives a single nod, as if he understands. Maybe he does. Dad always smiled and said these five are some of the smartest reindeer he's ever had, even if they're the most stubborn. Maybe they'll barrel their way through the room and knock those demons out or something. I share a long, tense look with him, and I swear I feel like he's trying to tell me something with his eyes.

My hand shakes as I walk back to the door, grab the doorknob, and turn. When I start to push it open, Cupid charges. I feel him knock into me, and I start to screech as I fall forward. But he doesn't let me hit the floor. His teeth close down on the white fur of my collar, and he lifts me up in his mouth until I dangle, my feet three inches above the floor as he bolts into the workshop.

I hear the thunder of the others' hooves as they all burst through the doorway.

My eyes travel over the normally beautiful space, full of arched windows with golden sills and floating workbenches spaced every five feet vertically so that cherubs can hover as they work. The walls are lined with gold shelves holding hundreds of thousands of magically miniaturized red and green wrapped gifts. But several of those shelves are broken. And the vibe in here is worse than the first body reveal in a slasher film, maybe because this is *real*.

Down at the end of the first row of workbenches, near the wood tools for carving trains, there are five cherubs chained together against the far wall, a demon holding a chainsaw hovering in front of them on gray wings.

Fuck.

My eyes travel over to Dad, who is battling two winged demons right now. They're locked together in combat, and bright flashes of red and white magic arc through the air.

Fear threatens to choke me, but then I hear Dad laugh. I relax a fraction of an inch, realizing that demons have tried to take over Christmas before. And they've always failed.

Dad will win, I tell myself firmly, trying to cement that authoritatively in my mind.

I just need to get out of his way so that I'm not a hindrance.

Comet's head jerks sideways, and I'm yanked to the right, another demon coming into view. This blue winged bastard burns our precious list of good girls and boys, cackling as the parchment turns to ash.

To his left is a roll-up garage door—the door we need. It's currently open, letting in moonlight and air cold enough to turn me into an ice sculpture in a matter of seconds. Standing in that doorway, surveying the scene with a grin, is a black-haired demon with at least seven red horns protruding from his head. The fucker is dressed up in an imitation Santa suit.

What an arrogant prick! Disdain bubbles up inside of me until that demon raises a hand and blasts the room with a surge of blue power.

Deep sadness rips through me, and it's worse than the cold. It's worse than the numb feeling that comes before frostbite. I want to curl up into a ball. I want to cry. I want to wrench out my hair and scream!

Despair garbles my vision and paints monsters where there were once only shadows. Every negative thought I ever had bursts up at once like zombies, all of them trudging towards me with ruthless energy, determined to destroy me.

There's a furious snort and a weird bellow behind me, and suddenly, Dasher is charging right at the fuck in the Santa suit. He lowers his horns and smashes into the demon, flinging the man out of the doorway, backwards into the sky.

I find myself swaying precariously, dangling by my dress from Cupid's mouth as he gallops forward through the workshop, streaking past half-stuffed teddy bears and doll heads that have been painted but not attached to bodies. I squeal and reach wildly with my hands, trying to hold on to anything. But before I can grab hold of something, he's leapt up high in the air, shooting through the now open doorway into the darkness.

And suddenly, we're flying.

The night sky surrounds me, and the frigid cold assaults my skin. My very lungs feel frozen when I take in a breath of the chilly night air.

"Comet!" I whisper, but my voice already sounds weak, every part of my body battling to keep me warm. The shivers commence, and they get more violent until I feel like my bones might splinter, crack, and rupture a vital organ.

Something presses against my back, and I startle, then look down. It's Donner. He's flying through the air just below Cupid, keeping pace, his back a warm inviting seat…

Cupid opens his mouth and drops me. I fall with a screech, right onto Donner's back.

I'm so frozen that my fingers can't latch on to his hair and I almost slide off, but luckily, Comet and Blitzen have taken up positions on either side of him and use their massive bodies to push me in the right direction until I finally get a good grip.

I've barely let out a sigh of relief when a *rat-a-tat-tat* sound reaches my ears.

Oh shit.

Those fuckers are shooting magic at us.

JOY

DONNER FLIES us until we reach the barn roof blossoming amid the snow banks and pine trees near the outskirts of our property like some wayward red flower. My heart is jumping like a child playing leapfrog as we begin our descent, landing in a blanket of wispy snow near the heavy barn door.

Fear for my dad consumes me as I stumble on shaky feet off of Donner's back. Comet and Blitzen both nuzzle my hands—almost as if they're attempting to comfort me—but I barely process their touch. It feels as if I'm trudging through oil, the dark liquid sticking to my skin and making my limbs leaden. Dad, the cherubs…

I feel faint, the events of the day rushing to my ears and causing them to pound.

Oh god. *Christmas.*

What's going to happen to Christmas?

I'm distantly aware of Cupid nudging me inside, where the air is immediately permeated with the musty odor of straw, days old shit, the dry musk of animal fur, and something akin to copper.

Dad.

Cherubs.

Christmas.

I try to remind myself that this shit happens all the time. Every demon murder wants to be the big bad who steal Christmas from the angels. And every single time, my dad defeats them with a jolly laugh. He loves to teach them a lesson in manners…by turning them into inanimate objects around the village. Candy Cane streetlights. Teddy bears. Hanging bulbs. After a century or two, Santa will release them from his magic and allow them a choice—spend another century in the North Pole as an inanimate object or go back to Hell. They *always* choose the latter.

But despite my belief in my father, I can still see his magical cane crashing against the workshop floor, his magic seeping from the snow globe in a wash of colors. How can he defeat the demons without that?

How? How? How?

I don't even realize that my feet are moving me towards the barn door, propelling me forward, until Dasher is in front of me, his antlered-head poking into my stomach. I swear that this reindeer looks pissed ninety-nine percent of the time. His dark, Bambi eyes are always slitted and rife with frustration.

I'm positive he growls at me, irritation radiating from his pores, as those dark eyes of his narrow further.

"Stop it, Dash!" I hiss as he continues to push me backwards, away from the barn door. The other four reindeer move until they're standing protectively in front of me, though Blitzen does immediately lay down, eyes hooded with sleep. "I need to help my dad!" I tell them.

My stomach is a tumultuous mixture of dread and anxiety as, outside the barn, I hear a startled cry and an ear-piercing scream. A cherub! I'm running again, practically barreling the reindeer over. Before I can make it more than a few steps, Cupid grabs the back of my apron and pulls me back behind them.

"Fucking reindeer," I hiss, though my ire isn't directed at them. No, the full-force of my anger is aimed at the demon murder attempting to harm my friends and family, while I'm helpless to do anything but twiddle my thumbs like a damsel in distress.

Well, fuck that. And fuck this. I'm not some princess in a tower who needs saving. Dad trained me—to think things through, to stand up for myself, and to fight my own battles. He may embody everything good and pure in the world, but me? His only daughter?

I'm very good at being naughty.

"Think, Joy, think," I mumble, beginning to pace behind the reindeer. They have turned to watch me, their heads tilted curiously to the side. All of them except for Blitzen, that is. He's already fast asleep, with Donner repeatedly jamming his hoof into the sleeping reindeer's snout. "What do you know?

I know that they're a demon murder, probably hoping to gain favor in Hell. They can only be killed if they have their Center with them, their fated mate, but I didn't see any female demon lurking around. Besides, most demons kill their Centers as soon as they find them in order to be impervious to harm. Why would they choose to be vulnerable when they can merely kill the love of their entire existence and be indestructible?

Yeah, stellar demon logic.

I swear, I'll never understand it.

"Okay, so they can't be killed…" I trail off as Blitzen releases a loud roar, jerking awake and kicking at Donner. Donner flashes me what I almost think is an impish grin as the two of them begin to roll around, their antlers scratching at each other's fur.

So, they can't be killed…

But my father deals with them every year…

I snap my fingers as the solution comes to me.

"The staff!" I say, pleased by my own epiphany. Turning towards Comet—the reindeer nearest to me, who is attempting to pull my gloves out of my coat pocket—I squeal, "We need to fix the staff!"

"Citizens of the North Pole!" a male voice booms from outside. The voice is loud, strident, and unfamiliar. Though I don't recognize it, icy fear skates down my spine and encases my heart.

I immediately race towards the nearest window, balancing precariously on a stack of hay, while the five reindeer flutter in the air around me.

Standing on the tallest snow hill, using a child's karaoke machine to amplify his voice—how the hell has he hooked it up to electricity? Is that his power?— stands one of the demons from earlier. This one has greasy blond hair that hangs longer in the front than the back, covering one eye completely. He's tall and lanky, but there's something about him that has my heart stuttering to a stop in fear. He just seems... dangerous. Evil. There's a malicious glint in his eyes that I've never seen before. Not once.

The rest of his demon murder spread out around him, their wings, horns, and talons on display. At their feet, trembling and sobbing, are some of the cherubs from the workshop. Almost all of them I recognize, and a cold wave of fury gathers inside of me. These are my *friends*. My family.

And currently, they're scared out of their minds, snot running down their faces and mingling with the tears already present.

"You are under new leadership!" the demon continues, gesturing towards two of his demons. I recognize the one with the hideous blue wings—let's call him Blue— and he's joined by an ugly man with a beak-like nose and copper hair. Between Ugly and Blue, his head lolling against his chest, is Santa.

"No," I breathe, terror squeezing my heart in an iron vise. I can barely breathe through it. My hands shake as dark spots dance in my vision. "Daddy?" I whimper, feeling young and small all over again. Feeling like that little girl who begged her father to check underneath her bed for demons and other monsters. The girl who worshiped the ground he walked on.

Cupid releases a tiny mewl, pressing his furry head against my palm, and I absently scratch behind his ears. But my eyes are fixated on the horrific sight before me.

Ugly and Blue drop Santa unceremoniously on the snow in front of the obvious murder leader...let's call him Bangs.

Bangs offers the cherubs a cruel, malevolent smirk. You ever heard the saying "capable of making angels weep?" Well, Bangs takes that to a whole new level. I'm not even near him, and I want to pee my pants, curl into a ball, and cry my eyes out, all in no particular order.

"As of now, Santa no longer runs this little shit show. The North Pole is under a new regime." Bangs kicks at Santa's stomach, and my father rolls over, allowing me to see his mottled face for the first time. I inhale sharply at the myriad of vicious green and blue bruises and deep cuts. He won't die—his Center passed away a long time ago, so he's not vulnerable—but he will be in pain until his magic heals him.

If his magic heals him.

I imagine the demons don't seem too keen on giving him the chance to get better.

What will they do to him? Torture him relentlessly?

And what about the cherubs?

What about *me*?

What about Christmas? All the faith and hope that it gives little children?

As of now, it appears that these demons don't know that I even exist, but I know my anonymity won't last. All they'll have to do is ask the cherubs—creatures who can't lie—specific questions concerning the residents of Christmas Village, and they'll have no chance but to spit it out.

I begin to step away from the window, from the image of my dad lying in a pool of his own blood. From the cherubs being cuffed and dragged back to the toy shop for…who the hell knows what.

The North Pole has been overrun, and I know that the cherubs won't lift a pudgy finger to save it. Sure, they're smart and wholesome and pure, but they're not fighters. They never have been, and they never will be. They've relied on Santa for centuries to protect the North Pole, and now that he's out of the way, not one of them will step up and be the leader we need them to be.

Which means it's up to me.

5

DEM, AKA COMET

I KNOW Joy is freaked out, but I'm pretty sure she's not quite as freaked out as us. Cal's face, if it were normal and not covered in stupid fur, would be as pale as an asscheek right now. Gus is pacing, his power wafting out in little bursts that make us all perk up in rage before he reels it back in. Even Bryn is awake, his dumbass sloth demon eyes wide open for once.

First off, the fact that Joy's in danger has me dancing nervously on my hooves. But second off, that was supposed to be us, dammit! We were supposed to get the drop on the big guy!

If we had, though, we would've never met Joy. Or worse…we might have killed her.

That thought shoves a lump into my throat the size of coal in a Christmas stocking.

Okay, fuck that. We shouldn't be those guys out there. My eyes travel over the figure of our mate. I always knew there was something special about her, but I didn't realize it was the mate thing. I can't always tell what I'm feeling in this reindeer body, because it has strange reactions. I picked on the guys when I took her flying, but it was shit I'd never have said if she could've understood me.

If Joy could hear my words and not some stupid near-mooing bullshit, I'd tell her that she's the most beautiful woman who's ever existed. I'd tell her that I dream about her, about showing her Hell and the secret burrow I made in the clouds to keep my stash.

I might even give her some of it. I stole a necklace off a rich English snob once that would look really beautiful on her.

I have a stash of stuff here too, but hiding things in the hay isn't nearly as effective as in the clouds. Back in Hell, no one could ever find my secret stolen treasures. Here, the ugly little cherubs rake out my stall every few days. I love making sure they find their own hats and scarves and things covered in my piss.

But I digress.

Joy's upset. As she should be. Christmas has just been stolen. I love stealing, but I hate getting robbed. And looking at her face right now is like staring at some precious, priceless vase that I snuck in and snagged, only to find out I cracked it and now it's broken. Something precious ruined.

Joy's precious. We can't let this ruin her.

"We should fucking attack them," I growl.

"Yeah, we should," Gus backs me up, pawing at the ground like a bull preparing to charge. His support doesn't make me feel as good as the others' would. A wrath demon will basically vote in favor of any opportunity to fight.

Nico says, "I don't know if we can take them."

I want to headbutt him, but that will draw attention, so instead, I just give him the stink eye, which doesn't work very well with these dumb, furry, semi-expressionless faces. Fuck, I miss eyebrows. A good crooked brow can communicate a hell of a lot.

"Just frustrating you. Can't help it," Nico adds quickly, so whatever pissed-reindeer expression I pulled off must have worked. "We should totally take them down, but I don't know about a direct attack."

"Attack with what? Our wet noses and hooves?" Bryn shakes his head. "I don't know, guys."

"You're just gonna let our mate lose her father, you lazy fuck?" I trot over and get in his face the best I can.

Bryn has always been the most beta of all of us. Being a sloth demon doesn't give him a lot of energy to compete against the alpha vibes most demons give off. He quickly hunches his shoulders when I get into his personal space. "No. I'm just…wondering how we can—"

"Everyone, shut up!" Cal interrupts, the comet-shaped white spot on his forehead wrinkling.

"What the fuck, dude?" Gus snorts at Cal, his anger making him so pumped up that if he doesn't blow off steam soon, he might attack one of us and not be able to help it. Sometimes, he just can't contain his anger. His nostrils flare, and he bares his teeth. "Why the fuck are you telling us what to fucking do?"

"Maybe because you all got so busy debating what you wanted that you forgot about our mate!" Cal retorts. He's never been afraid to go toe to toe with Gus. I have to hand it to Cal—the demon's got big balls. If he bedazzled them, he could help New York City ring in the New Year.

"Don't lie. We've been thinking about her this whole time," Bryn argues.

"Yeah, then where is she?" Cal snaps.

My head turns so fast that my antlers get snagged on Nico's. "Shit!" We untangle—it's not our first rodeo—and scan the barn.

But Joy is gone. Only a set of footprints are left, a trail in the snow from the barn towards the outskirts of the village, an area we've never been to before.

"Well, shit," Gus exclaims.

Yeah, that about sums it up.

Cal immediately starts out after the prints, trudging through the snow, muttering dumb lies like, "She'll catch her death of cold." She won't. She's half-angel. But when he gets agitated, it gets hard for Cal to tell the truth.

The others trot after him, but I look around the barn, eyes searching for anything I could take that might help us later. There's a pitchfork near a pile of hay, but despite common stereotypes, we don't all learn how to wield those. There are saddles and toolboxes that I have no chance of carrying since all I can use is my mouth.

But then I see a rope. We could use a rope, right? Maybe Joy can douse it in gasoline, and then we can lasso those fuckers and set them on fire. They won't die, but I'm pretty sure they'll have to rethink their life choices long enough for the cherubs and Santa to get the jump on them.

Pleased with myself, I jump up onto the top of a stall door, using my front paws to hold myself up as I remove a big coil of rope from the barn wall. Then, I hop down and trot happily after the rest of my murder, daring rescue plots dancing like sugarplums in my head.

In my imagination, the guys and I weave the rope into a net with our tongues, using our very underused cherry-stem-tying skills. Then, we fly as reindeer and drop the net on the other demons, freeing Santa. He's so happy that he turns us back into demons again. And once he's turned those other assholes into reindeer or whatever the hell he wants, I take the leftover rope to Joy and let her tie me up for playtime.

I'm about to spill my very brilliant plan to the guys when I realize where we are. We're past the forest, and we've broken through the lightest veil between realms that's ever existed. We're in Heaven.

Ohhh shit. I glance over my shoulder, suddenly scared that God's right behind me, about to scold me or smite me or who knows what.

I've never set foot in Heaven before. Some demons do…in war, on a dare, just for a laugh. I've never been one of them. Christmas Village is as close as I've ever come, because who wants to be stuck around uptight goody two shoes all the time? Blech. That sounds about as appealing as oatmeal. Which, I'm never eating again, by the way. Once I'm not a reindeer, oats and carrots will no longer be a part of my daily diet. Ever. I might even find some demonic ritual that burns them just for the sake of defacing them.

I almost drop the rope in my mouth as I stare around at Heaven. It's set in the clouds, just like Hell. But unlike Thieves' Tower, where I grew up, the clouds here aren't black and full of lightning that can burn your hand if you don't steal quickly enough. There's no trick fog that you can step in, thinking it's a solid cloud, where you end up sunken to the waist, prime pickings for any other thievery demon. Everything here is so...bright.

It's like I've stepped onto a movie set and there are thirty spotlights on me. That's how much damn white there is. White little huts that look like dollops of whipped cream circle around a courtyard just in front of us. In the center of that courtyard is a fountain made of ice that spits out pretty little snowflakes that drift down slowly.

Ugh.

It's annoyingly pretty and cutesy. I used to think Christmas Village was bad, but over the years, I've gotten used to it. *This* is just overkill. There's not a speck of smog in these clouds. Where's the bird shit dropping down from above? It's too white.

I notice the reindeer in front of me—probably Gus, though I'm not that skilled in telling a reindeer by his ass—leave brown tracks on the clouds, and that gives me a twisted sense of satisfaction. Yeah. Take that, Heaven. Not so perfect now, are you?

We trot past houses that have hearts for windows, then some that have shamrocks. What the hell is this? Lucky Charms Village? Are there going to be rainbows and balloons next? The final few houses have stars in the windows, and I nearly laugh at how accurate my mockery is.

I spot a llama wandering the streets nearby, and I have to stifle the urge to charge at him. Heaven and their stupid llamas. Santa's always threatening to replace us with them when we don't do something perfectly. My hoof paws the cloudy ground, and the llama turns towards me, narrowing his eyes and widening his stance.

Ohhhh, that's definitely a challenge.

I square up against him and inhale, ready to charge— until I see the fuzzy fucker belch fire. A bright orange ball forms in front of him and swirls a few feet closer to me before dropping into the clouds and extinguishing with a hiss of steam.

What the fuck?

Are they supposed to be able to do that?

Cal snorts, drawing my attention away from the llama that I'm pretty sure is trying to cause drama. Fucking drama llamas. I turn and watch as Joy slips inside a house on the far side of the courtyard.

"Come on, guys. We have to protect her!" He gallops forward.

White lie.

Angels and half-angels don't need protection in Heaven.

But because I'm a team player, and because I'm suddenly itching to steal something from an angel, I follow along.

We push inside the little hut, and Joy squeaks with surprise when she sees us. "Boys!" Her hand flies to her chest. "What are you doing here?"

Cal just shoves his forehead under her hand so she can pet him. It's the only possible answer we can give that she'll understand.

Behind Joy, a chubby cherub, who's as wide as he is tall, flutters in from the other room, carrying a teapot and two cups on a tray. His loincloth is stretched quite tight over his...area. He probably needs to give in and buy the next size up. His tummy shakes like a bowl full of jelly when he spots us. "Oh! Oh my! How cute!"

Cute, my ass. I exchange an annoyed look with Nico. I don't even bother to glance at Gus, because I know that statement will have pissed the wrath demon off.

"I didn't realize I had extra visitors!" the cherub exclaims.

I swear to Lucillania that if he starts cuddling me or petting me, I'm sticking my antlers into his belly folds.

Joy smiles ruefully. "I'm sorry, Elyon. I didn't realize these little boogers had followed me."

Little boogers. Ew. If she only knew…that would be the last pet name she'd give us. I wonder if I could get her to call me Daddy…

"Well, I don't have any carrots right now." Elyon sighs in disappointment.

"Oh, don't worry. I give these guys lots of cookies. They're fine." Joy waves a hand and glances at me. "Apparently, Comet is snacking on a rope right now." She laughs lightly before she sighs and sits down on the cherub's plush white couch while he sets out the tea service on the coffee table. My girl wrings her fingers as she waits politely for him to pour. Angels have this patience that would never fucking fly in Hell. I don't get it.

My eyes start wandering the room, wondering if I could fit one of those silver teaspoons in my mouth and still carry the rope without choking myself. But my head whips back to Joy when she speaks after taking that required first sip of peppermint-scented tea. "I did come to see you for a very important reason. Dad's Christmas cane is broken. I need to know how to fix it."

6

JOY

ELYON BLINKS, surprised. "Is something wrong in Christmas Village? Did the demons actually—"

"No," I quickly lie. Why? Because the last time demons took over a holiday realm, they corrupted Saint Patrick's Day and turned it into a drunken mess on Earth, not to mention the war that went on between the angels and demons for centuries afterwards. My dad lost his Center during that war, as well as the rest of his flock.

I can't let anything like that start up again.

I fish around for possible explanations. I notice Blitzen's about to fall asleep in the corner, his horns precariously close to the star-shaped windows on the walls of Elyon's little hut. "Um. Blitzen did it. He's got narcolepsy or something. Yeah, he's always half asleep, and he fell over. Smash." I give a desperate chuckle as I gesture at the reindeer, and Elyon eyes him suspiciously.

Blitzen just lets out a snore as he falls asleep standing up.

"You know, I get a weird feeling from these reindeer," the old cherub says, rubbing absently at his chest.

"I know! They're the sweetest, aren't they?"

He quirks a brow at me, like he can't believe I just said that.

Well, fine. Maybe it's not normal for most angels to be best friends with reindeer, but I'm not most angels. I'm half-human. There are plenty of humans whose best friend is an animal. So there. I mentally stick my tongue out at him.

Aloud, I say, "I've kind of adopted them. But that's beside the point. The Christmas cane. I need to know what to do about it. Before…err…before my dad discovers what happens. Because he'll be mad, you know? Can you help? Pretty please, with a Christmas tree star on top?"

Elyon takes a sip of his tea, eyeing me closely. I try to sit patiently and not squirm like I just lied my ass off.

Dad always used to be able to tell when I lied as a little girl. Apparently, I had a *tell*. A shifty eye, my dad would say. I would always look at his forehead whenever I lied. But my techniques have improved since then, because the overweight cherub sighs and nods. He was Santa's second-hand man before he retired here two decades ago, and he knows everything Christmas. I always considered him the strict older uncle, one I only saw on occasion but still felt I could trust. "Hold on. Let me go find the book."

I wait until he's out of the room to clap my hands and then hug the reindeer who's nearest. It happens to be Dasher. "Yes! Oh, thank goodness!"

Dasher's tongue sneaks out and licks the shell of my ear, and I bat him away playfully. "Ew. Gross. Save that for the stable. I'm sure Prancer or Vixen would like it."

Dasher immediately makes a moan of protest. Or maybe it's agreement. I can't really tell as I wipe down my ear with my sleeve and turn back to pay attention to Elyon, who re-enters the room carrying a heavy, leather tome.

I lean forward as he sits down beside me, the tips of his wings brushing against my sides when he opens the book. He licks a finger and flicks through several pages until he finds what he's looking for. He taps a hand-drawn image of a Christmas staff, and I lean in, fascinated.

He clears his throat before saying, "Here we are. Now, let's see what it says… Oh, there! The staff must be fashioned from a branch from the tree of knowledge. Oh, that'll be in that abandoned garden of Eden. Should be easy enough to get, though a bit overgrown. God hasn't really gone in there since the *incident*. For magic, you'll need innocence… Oh, those will be sweet little moments. The River of Innocence is just a short flight north. We dip all the souls in there before they're born on the various planets. Just scoop up a bit of that water, and you should be set."

"Easy enough." I stand, anxious to get to it, but Elyon's arm shoots out, stopping me short.

"Wait. Please." He turns the page. "That's not all you need."

"It's not?" I ask, my stomach sinking as I sit back down. I feel time ticking away like there's a bomb in Christmas Village. Technically, we *are* on a countdown. If I don't get rid of these demons soon, we might not be able to fix Christmas. Suddenly, I'm irrationally annoyed at Dad for not keeping a spare cane around. I take a deep breath and exhale slowly, trying to let that emotion leak away. It's not his fault. "What else do I need?"

"It says here that Christmas is also a time of joy, so you'll need to grab some joy."

I nod. "Okay. Is there a river or somewhere I can stop at to get that?"

"Oh, no." Elyon shakes his head. "You'll have to be more clever to collect joy. It's a trickier thing."

Well, that was non-specific and utterly unhelpful, I think as I fake a smile. "Okay, but still. You know how to get it, right?"

"The most guaranteed way to collect it is to be present for a first kiss between two individuals. If you say the words, 'Venit Gaudium' just before they kiss one another for the first time, then you should be able to collect it. But first kisses are terribly hard to witness. Most are done in private."

I scrub a hand over my eyes. "Well, I don't really have a choice. Okay, fine. Got it. Three things."

"Four."

"Four things? Four?! What's the *fourth* thing?" I am exasperated. In about two seconds, I'm gonna grab that book from Elyon and rip out the pages I need. I don't care if he's practically an uncle twice removed.

"Well…the glass dome on top of the cane must be made from the glass of a storm in Hell. I… Oooh, yikes!" His white eyebrows spring up.

"I'm sorry, what's that?" I ask, lost. I have, obviously, never been to Hell. "What's a glass storm?"

Elyon blinks at me for a second. "Why don't you take another sip of tea…"

When he tells me what a glass storm is, how molten glass just shoots down from the clouds of Hell at random and can strip the very skin from your body, I can't help it. I don't care that I'm currently in Heaven. I let out a loud, shocked, "Holy fuck!"

WE STAND OUTSIDE THE GARDEN OF EDEN, HAVING USED a hand-drawn map Elyon made us in order to navigate here. The area is a walled enclosure, and the walls are made of ice blocks, cold and white and intimidating.

Despite its unfriendly exterior, I'm glad we're here. Finally. It took three tries, even with a map, because clouds fucking look the same from above. At least in Christmas Village, there are actual mountains to the east so that you can always reference them, even amongst the endless white blanket of snow.

We land outside of a golden gate that shines pristinely, despite the fact that it's wrapped in a metric ton of black vines. I slide off of Comet's back so I can try the latch, but no matter how I yank, I can't get it open.

I end up breaking a nail and wailing, yelling, "Dammit!"

A second later, I see Dasher running straight at the gate. He rams it with his horns but only manages to get one of them stuck.

He brays like a donkey when that happens, and for a second, I wonder if it hurts reindeer when their horns get scraped. I thought they were only bone, but who knows?

"Shh, it's okay, Dash. It's okay, sweetie." I speak softly and pat his neck as I carefully guide his head so he can free his antlers. "There." I kiss my finger and bop his nose. "Thank you for trying to help me."

He makes noises like he thinks he's actually responding to me, and it's so darn cute that I have to smother a laugh. I nod seriously as if I can understand him. "You're right. That's the meanest gate in the whole universe."

Behind me, the other reindeer snort and chuff.

I turn to glare at them. "Don't make fun of Dasher. He got a boo boo."

This does not seem to convince them to stop. Blitzen even falls to the ground, snorting and kicking as his chest heaves.

"Whatever, Dash. Let's fly on in there and get that stick." I put a comforting hand on his neck. He lets me climb onto him and then shoots the rest of the reindeer

deer a look, something I would almost describe as smug, before we hop in a perfect arc over the gate and into the overgrown garden.

Ew. For being a part of Heaven, it's icky in here. There are gray vines all over the place, like the plants just lost hope and shriveled up to die. Most of the vegetation looks dead, bushes empty of leaves. There are no flowers. The only things growing in here seem to be a massive red vine that slithers through the garden like a snake, branching off and spreading around until it almost looks like this garden is part of some anatomy project on the circulatory system.

Besides the vine, only a huge tree in the middle of the garden is left.

The Tree of Knowledge is not dead like the other plants here. It looks vivacious and healthy. Its trunk is as wide as Dad's sleigh, and crisp leaves unfurl like little green stars from its branches.

"Can you hover?" I ask Dash, and he obediently kicks back up into the air and then floats next to one of the outer branches of the tree. My eyes roam over it until I find the perfect branch. Then I reach out and yank on it. Of course, the branch is strong and the tree is thriving, so the wood is supple and doesn't break. "Oh, come on! I really need a piece of you." I grunt as I pull harder.

"What the heck!" a voice booms, and I'm so startled that I nearly fall off Dasher's back. Who was that? Is someone after us? Is it one of the demons, coming to stop me from fixing the cane? How did they know I was here?

The branch I'm pulling on curls and flicks me and Dash, sending us hurtling backwards through the air. Luckily, Dash rights us just in time for us to hear, "How dare you just attack me!"

I realize with a jolt that this tree has a face in its trunk. What I thought was a knot was actually a nose. Two giant eyes have opened, and what looked like a crooked saw cut in the trunk is actually a mouth that's moving. It's not evil demons speaking to me. It's...it's the tree! "Why in all the worlds would you just try and break me?"

My hand flies to my chest. "I'm sorry! No one told me you were sentient!"

"Of course I'm sentient, you imbecile. How else could I be a tree of *knowledge*?" he huffs, flickering his branches almost as if he's dusting his shoulder off.

"Oh. Um. Right." Elyon soooooo did not prepare me for this. Backlit by the rising sun, the talking tree looks even more eerie, the sunrise painting the bark in shades of pink and orange. I'm sure there's a joke about morning wood that I can make, but I'm too freaked out

81

to think. "Look, I was told I need a branch from you in order to make a Christmas magic cane."

"I thought there already was one of those," the tree retorts.

"It broke?" This accidentally comes out as a question.

"You're *not sure?*" His sarcasm is as rough as bark.

"I *am* sure. I just need one branch, please…"

He narrows his eyes, and there's a long, drawn-out moment where he no doubt senses my desperation. "Okay, fine. Just tell me what branch of knowledge you need, and you can have it." He smiles, and it's not a nice one. Can trees even have nice smiles? Fuck, why am I overthinking this?

"Oh, any old branch is great." I try to appease him. "Even a dead one will do."

"Dead branches of knowledge… You mean like alchemy?" His expression crinkles. "Here's a secret I don't tell most people. I don't have dead branches."

"Um…well…I don't really know what you're talking about." I'm super lost.

"Name a branch, and I'll give it to you," he says again, and this time, I'm certain his smile is condescending. It kinda makes me want to use weed killer on this fucker.

"I have to name a branch. Do they already have names?" Does he name his branches the way some of the dragon shifters down at the pub name their biceps 'fire' and 'flame'? Is this some kind of weird guy thing?

"Of course they have names…you uneducated fool!" Wow. Hurtful. Ignoring that. "There are six branches of knowledge. Philosophy, humanities, mathematics —YEOWWWWW!"

The Tree of Knowledge screeches as a crack sounds through the garden. Comet suddenly shoots up from behind the tree, a rope gripped in his teeth, a branch dangling from one end with the rope tied snuggly around it. Dang! I didn't even see him sneak in here. He was as quick as Santa!

"Come back! Thief!" the tree yells.

Comet jerks his head at me and Dasher in a frantic 'follow me' gesture, before jetting out of the garden.

Dasher doesn't waste time. We shoot up into the sky like a rocket as the tree bellows after us, "You idiots! You took a branch from mathematics! Good luck with that! You're too stupid to know—"

My reindeer group around me and all start to bray, drowning out the tree as we get farther away. It almost sounds like they are praising Comet.

"Thank you, Comet," I say sincerely. "Well, I'm glad that strange encounter is over." I blow out a breath. "Good thing you all can't talk, because I'm pretty sure one of you would make a snarky comment about how we're about to go snag some 'innocence water' after we just stole something." A shiver races down my spine. But it's not the scared kind. It's the thrilled kind. I've never stolen anything before.

But it's for a good cause, right?

The existence of Christmas Village and the happiness of children all over Earth depend on it.

And besides, a reindeer took the branch. I mean, technically, animals can't steal, right? They don't know the rules.

Yup, I'm sticking with that logic.

We fly through the sky for about ten minutes before we spot a golden river snaking through the clouds, the banks reflecting a bright yellow light. We dip down towards the water before I realize something.

"Oh, no! I didn't bring a cup!" I sigh at myself, utterly frustrated as I stare around, looking to see if there are angels nearby I can ask for help or anything. There aren't. There's nothing but the river itself and clouds.

Blitzen puts on a burst of speed that I've never seen from him before. He splashes right down into the river and scoops up a bunch of water in his mouth, before rolling and splashing in it like a puppy. We land on the banks and watch him. I chuckle for a second, and when Dash lands, I walk down to the bank and call Blitzen over. He trots over with a smile on his face and bulging cheeks.

He's totally trying to carry the water we need in his mouth, sweet boy.

My heart lifts seeing that, but I'm worried he'll fall asleep and choke himself. We need something else. I could soak a bit of my skirt. But if I do that, I might end up soaking too much. And then what if I get cold when we fly? I can't even begin to count the number of lectures I've gotten over the years about the dangers of wet clothing and cold weather. It takes a second, but soon, my mind lights up with an alternative. "Blitz, I'm gonna have to ask you to do something a little weird, ok?"

He nods solemnly, or as solemnly as one can when their cheeks are puffed out like chipmunk's.

"Can you come here?" I prop an arm on his side when he moves closer. I use him to balance myself as I pull up my skirt and yank my panties down, pulling them carefully off over my boots. Blitz's head has swiveled to stare at me intensely.

No, that can't be right. Not intensely, I correct myself as I fix my skirt. *He just has no clue what's going on.* "Can you dip these in the water and then carry them in your mouth for me? That way we have water, but it's not quite so…"

Blitz opens his mouth, and the water inside cascades out as he leans forward and snags the panties out of my hand quickly.

Behind me, I hear a low moan from one of the other reindeer. "Just a sec," I call, not looking back. They're probably getting impatient waiting.

Blitz trots back out into the water and lets my lacy white panties dip down into the golden water. Then he pulls them back up and nods at me.

"Two items down, boys. Now, who wants to give me a ride to get the next item on our list?"

There's practically a stampede to get to me.

WHEN WE FLY INTO HELL, THE FIRST THING I'M SHOCKED by is that it's only a bit different from Heaven. Until I see a canyon in the clouds and peer down into it.

I quickly jerk my eyes up, unable to process the unspeakable things happening down there. So. Many. Dicks. And boobs. And whips. And whips made of fire.

And whips with nails at the end. And whips made entirely of floppy dildos. And is that…is that a sex swing made of human intestines?

"Okay, so we are definitely not touching down here." I'm pretty sure Comet made a sad, disappointed braying noise. "Be careful, and keep your eyes peeled for molten glass," I command.

Donner, who ended up winning the race amongst the reindeer, shifts underneath me. He's been doing that a lot. I'm not sure if it's because I'm riding without panties and it feels different to him. It certainly feels different to me. If I'd known there was going to be this much sensation, I think I might have risked the wet skirt.

I grab his horn and lean forward, trying to make out something in the distance. "Is that it?" I ask, pointing at a red blob.

Donner very definitively shakes his head no, and all the reindeer veer away from the red blur in the distance. Hmmm…I wonder if reindeer have great eyesight.

Suddenly, my reindeer goes into a dive that leaves me shrieking and clinging on for dear life. He lands amidst a group of demon children who have bright orange wings and tiny horns the size of pencils on their foreheads. They appear to be on a platform of wispy red clouds that spark as if with lightning bolts. Tiny metallic nails protrude from some of the clouds closest to me, though the demon children appear unperturbed, as if they deal with erratic nail-clouds all the time.

The kids are involved in what looks like a game of marbles. They scatter when we land in the middle of their game.

"Oh! I love marbles! We make them all the time at the workshop." I clap. It takes a second before I realize why Donner landed here. Oh, he's a genius. These are probably made of Hell glass!

One of the kids, a little black-haired imp, raises his eyebrows. "You wanna play? You gotta bet."

I shrug. "I'm afraid I don't have anything to bet." I stare longingly down at the marbles. I really need some of those. Dammit.

"You got a dress, don't you?" The demon kid gives me a grin that suddenly makes me wonder if these demons are children after all. Maybe they're the cherub version of a demon…eternally small and child-like.

"How old are you?" I ask.

"Three-hundred and seventy-two," he responds instantly.

But he has a snarky grin on his face. The kind that I used to get when I lied to Dad. He can't be more than fifty, which is basically a demon preschooler.

Granted, he's still way older than me and is kinda looking like he wants to eat me alive, but still. "Lie!" I call him out.

That's a bad idea. Because suddenly, his wings are flared, and this fucker has fangs, and all of his little friends group around behind him.

Apparently, he doesn't like when I out him in front of his friends. Oops?

Donner lowers his head and charges. And then, just as his antlers toss the first demon up, he lets a huge fart rip. The other demons groan and cover their noses. He bucks wildly, dancing all around, making noises I've never heard him make before.

What. The. Fuck?

I'm shocked into silence for a moment, before Cupid comes closer and nudges my shoulder with his nose. Oh, right. Marbles.

I lean down and scoop up a handful, hoping that's enough. Then I climb onto Cupid's back. Seconds later, we're soaring through the sky away from those demons. I'm not sure why they don't follow until Donner joins us and the stench is so disgusting, I have to cover my nose. That would be why.

But I'm grateful. Without him, we definitely wouldn't have been able to distract those demons and get away.

Now, we've checked three items off our list. Only one to go.

I open my hand to stare down at my palm. I can't blame stealing these on a reindeer. Guilt creeps across my chest. I'll have to send those demon children some presents. Or maybe some cookies. Even evil creatures love cookies, right?

I nod to myself as I harden my resolve. We have to complete this mission, and fast. We only have one thing left to do.

"Let's get to Earth!" I call out to the reindeer.

We need to go interrupt a first kiss.

I WANT TO CRY. I WANT TO RIP MY HAIR OUT. WE'VE tried and failed to interrupt three different kisses. I guess appearing in front of humans and chanting Latin words is kind of a turn off.

Who knew?

Gah! I stomp into the closest bakery, needing to gorge my sorrows on sugar. "One second, guys," I tell the reindeer, leaving them on the sidewalk, much to the curiosity of random passersby.

The bakery is a cheery sort of place, despite the fact that it's yellow and pink color scheme feels all wrong. I miss my kitchen. That's where I belong, not out scouring the realms to collect ingredients for stupid Christmas canes.

I feel tears gather in the corner of my eyes, and I blink them back quickly, determined not to cry.

I spot some creme brûlée, a desert I love but rarely make because Dad doesn't really like it. I point at the dessert and sniff, fighting off a good self-pity sob.

The guy behind the counter gives me a smile. He's clean-cut and young, his hair cropped close to his head. He's not breathtaking, but his smile is sweet and sincere, which I really need after this incredibly difficult day.

"Good choice," the bakery guy says, opening the back of the display case and sliding a mini creme brûlée into a plastic dessert container before snapping it shut. It's not until the guy moves to the register that I realize I don't have any human money.

The sobs that I was holding back start up with a vengeance. They're loud and horrifying, manifesting all of my worry about Dad and the cherubs and the workshop. People outside probably think that I'm insane.

The bakery guy hurries around the counter with the treat. "Miss, are you okay?"

I shake my head and swipe at my eyes, trying to stop the tears. "I don't have any money."

"Shhh, it's all right. It's all right." He rubs a comforting hand up and down my back. "This will be on the house."

Awww. How sweet! I mop up my eyes, making sure they're completely dry, because a thank you smile that's halfway to a sob is pretty pathetic.

A crash against the door makes us both jerk up and turn in surprise. Comet's antlers are pressed against the glass, and he's craned his neck to look in.

Shoot. He must have heard me crying and thought I was getting hurt.

"Holy shit!" bakery guy exclaims.

I glance at his name tag and read "Ben." That's a nice name.

Ben leans back from me and runs a hand over his cropped hair. "I gotta call animal control!"

"No! Don't! Please!" I shoot towards him, my face now precariously close to Ben's. "He's with me." I totally forgot that humans don't just walk around town with animals all the time. In Christmas Village, everyone uses reindeer. It's the fad, as the kids these days say.

Yes, I'm still in my twenties, but that doesn't make me a kid. Shut up.

"What?" Confusion is scribbled across the poor guy's features as he glances between me and Comet.

"We're…part of a Christmas exhibit," I lie, thinking quickly. "But, um, my boyfriend broke up with me. Called me a bad kisser in front of everyone!"

Ben's eyes widen, and I can tell he believes me, which only feeds this little lie monster inside of me.

I gesture wildly with my box of dessert in one hand. "Yeah, even my dad heard. It was the most humiliating experience of my entire life! I never want to see him again." I finish with a dramatic head turn, staring down and to the side like movie stars always do during their intense scenes.

"What an asshole!" Ben exclaims.

I force out a little laugh, pleased when my tight throat makes it breaks so I sound truly heartbroken. I could move to Earth and win an Oscar.

Maybe. If I pull this off. Because, suddenly, I have a plan. I'm getting that joy magic, dammit, or my name's not Joy.

I fake swipe at my eyes as if they aren't completely dry now. Then I stare plaintively up at Ben. "Will you tell me if I'm a bad kisser?"

"What?"

He's not the brightest bulb on the Christmas tree.

"Would you kiss me and tell me if it's true?" I beg.

"I…uh…I…"

I take a step closer. He thinks I'm crazy, but his eyes keep dipping down my figure, meaning he's not quite sure what he wants to do.

I gently grab hold of his shirt. "Please?" I softly whimper.

His head dips down towards mine, and I whisper the Latin words I need under my breath. Then I close my eyes, purse my lips, and lean up on my tiptoes. I'm so focused on my goal that I only dimly hear a dozen bells ringing accompanied by the stomp of hooves.

All of a sudden, my lips touch something warm…and furry.

I pull myself backwards, startled to see Comet, not Ben, in front of me. I just kissed my reindeer on the cheek!

What the hell happened—

I stop questioning things when I realize that in the air, right between Comet and me, is a red snowflake, glistening and floating in midair. I quickly open my bakery box and lift it up until I can trap that snowflake. Then I snap the lid shut.

Fuck. If I'd known it could be any old first kiss, even to a pet, I would have been done with this part hours ago. Curse Elyon and his very under-descriptive book.

"Thanks, boy," I whisper to Comet.

He blinks dreamily at me.

"The Health Department's gonna kill me!" Ben exclaims, standing up from the ground somewhere behind me. Oops. I guess Comet knocked him over.

I jerk my head towards the door. "No. We're leaving. I'm so sorry, Ben! You're a really sweet guy! Thanks for the dessert! Sorry about the kiss!" My apologies are rushed and hurried as we run out the front of the little shop and join the rest of my little herd of heroes.

"All right, boys! We got it!" A Christmas-morning-sized grin expands across my face. "Let's go build a cane and save Christmas!

7

JOY

I AM gonna shove so much Christmas magic into those
evil demons that they'll shit bows and burp sparkles.
Or something equally ridiculous.

New cane in hand, I turn toward my loyal reindeer. We
snuck into the workshop under the cover of darkness
to take some tools—Comet is really a sneaky shit, I
gotta give him that—and then built our own little snow
fort out in the evergreen forest. All last night, we
huddled together under the moonlight, working to
assemble the brand-new Christmas cane that is now
clutched in my hand.

I know Rudolph always gets all the credit on Earth, but
really, these guys are the sweetest little pets ever. They

helped me all night long, and Blitzen only laid down to sleep once.

I pat each one on the head, rubbing my cheek against every reindeer's one at a time, giving them thank you snuggles. They deserve it. Every one of them contributed to getting those ingredients.

After the cuddle-fest, I take a deep breath and try to amp myself up for a showdown. But man is it hard not to quake in your boots when the only showdown you've ever done was a bake-off against some cherubs in an attempt to replicate *The Great British Baking Show*.

I mean, Dad is the badass. Not me. He's the one who's fought off demons for centuries. Not me.

Which is why I know exactly what we need to do.

"Okay, guys, my goal is to get this cane to Dad, so he can whip some demon ass." I gesture at the cane as if they understand me, but hey, they're all the team I've got right now, so I'm going with it. "Do you think that you could maybe distract those guys while Dasher runs me to Dad?" My eyes fall on Donner. He was awfully good at distracting and annoying those kids. For some reason, I feel like this sort of thing is in his wheelhouse. He can fart on them all he wants to. Let his freak flag fly. Let the stink bombs explode. Let the—

You get the idea.

Donner gives me a single nod.

"Let's do this! Gah! I feel like we need red and green war paint and maybe 'Eye of the Tiger' playing in the background." I crack my neck like that's going to serve some sort of badass purpose. Then I climb onto Donner's back. At this point, I hardly even notice that I'm not wearing panties anymore.

"On Dasher and Donner. On Blitzen, Comet, and Cupid! Let's go make these demons look really stupid!" I call out.

They kick off, and we soar into the sky in a perfect line, with military precision. We are gonna be so amazing at this.

WHOMP.

A gray-winged demon appears out of nowhere and slams into me and Donner, making us roll.

I cling on, my hands and feet wrapping monkey-style around the reindeer as he struggles to right us. As soon as I can think clearly again, I'm pissed the hell off.

What the fuck? Is that guy an unpleasant surprise demon? Those fuckers always try to mess up gift giving. I didn't know they could become invisible.

I'm seriously regretting that every book I own right now is a cookbook. I have so much to research about reindeer and demons.

Right after I survive.

The gray-winged demon pops up next to me again, his creepy white eyes only divided by a snake-like pupil. They focus right on the Christmas cane in my hands.

Crap.

"Dive!" I shout to Donner as Dasher body slams the demon in midair. But it doesn't matter what I yell, because even as we speed towards the snow, I see two more demons fly out of the workshop to meet us.

My heart starts pounding with anticipation, like the moment before someone unwraps your gift and you're worried that they'll hate it. It's not a good feeling.

Blitzen brays louder than I've ever heard him before as he barrels into one of the two blue-winged demons heading for us. He bites the demon's hand with a vicious streak I never thought he possessed. And then he whips his head back and forth like a wild dog tearing into its prey.

The demon howls in pain, and I...cheer. My human side eclipses my angelic one, and for a moment, all I care about is that my reindeer are winning.

Comet and Cupid both fly straight at the second demon heading our way, kicking their hooves out and nailing him in the wings so that he screeches and goes pinwheeling through the sky as he falls.

"Quick, we need to get this cane to Dad!" I whisper to Donner. "We have to find him."

Quick as a flash, we dash away from the fight and towards the workshop. I hope like hell that Dad's being kept in the workshop and not in some strange spot somewhere in the village, or we'll never find him.

One of the roll-up garage doors to the workshop is open, and light twinkles from inside, cheery and bright. But it's deceiving. Nothing will be happy again until Santa's back.

We fly inside and zoom past the bear-stuffing machine that looks like a giant cotton ball dispenser. We zigzag around the plastic parts of Power Wheels cars that are mid-assembly. No one's there. Anywhere. The workshop is a ghost town.

I've never seen it more creepy. I swear that the clown from *It* could pop out from behind some of the puppets that are currently suspended from the ceiling, and I wouldn't even be surprised. Freaked out, yes, but not surprised.

I can see some of the demon's progress already. Quite a few of the toys have been altered into Frankenstein-style mish-mashes that will scare the shit out of any kid who unwraps it. Most of the dolls and bears have had their eyeballs ripped out and replaced with blinking red lights.

Fuck.

I love horror movies. When they're on TV. But living one? Being part of an Earth-wide nightmare? No thank you.

My eyes scan the room, searching for any kind of clue as to where Dad is. If we can just give him the cane...

I spot a red thread trailing along the floor.

Did Dad unravel his suit and leave it like a breadcrumb trail? Did he hope that someone would come to help? Did he leave it for me?

I'm not even sure he saw me escape last time, but the idea that Dad might have left me a clue latches on, and I can't shake it.

If I've learned one thing from living with Christmas year-round, it's that people need hope. And right now, that little red string on the floor is feeding me hope that my dad is in here somewhere, conscious enough to be waiting for his rescue.

"The door to the ball room!" I whisper and point for Dasher, realizing he won't know what I'm talking about if I just say the name.

He flies silently over to the bright green door that leads to where we keep all the balls we make. We used to keep them in the main room of the workshop, but whenever one would get loose, it was a disaster, tripping cherubs or bouncing into their paint pots. About a decade ago, they added a separate room for ball handlers.

I give a wistful smile, because the innocent little cherubs didn't even realize how dirty that job description sounded.

We get close to the door, which has a little window above the handle. I lean over and try to peer in as Dash attempts to hover in place.

But it's so dark. I can't see. I start to slide off when a rush of air hits my cheeks. I pause what I'm doing and turn.

A demon with horns that look as sharp as knives snatches me from Donner's back before I can take a breath and scream. I recognize him as the one I nick-named Ugly, with the beak-like nose and copper hair.

His hands have turned into claws, and those sharp nails dig into the skin of my sides where he holds me.

My heart thuds so loudly, I think I might go deaf as my hands scrabble to clutch onto him, so that the asshole can't just drop me on my head.

He gives off an evil laugh and whispers in my ear, "Well, aren't you a pretty little thing. I think I might take you and make sure you get on the naughty list."

Black dread floods my system, and I feel like I'm drowning in oil, toxic sludge creeping over my skin with every touch.

Yes, I saw those demon kids in Hell. They were malicious, sure, and maybe even cruel, but I don't think I've ever faced pure evil before now.

But this man…

He's pure evil.

I freeze, terrified, and the demon laughs at my distress as he glides back out the door of the workshop and up into the sky, where my reindeer are still battling the other fiends. Donner is beneath us, attempting to lunge for me, but this demon is ten times faster than him, which is hella fast, considering these reindeer pull Dad around the globe in a single night.

We accelerate, and he shoots up fifty feet into the air. I cringe, and my hands claw desperately at his forearms, certain now that his plan is to drop me. As my hands twist, I lose my grip…and the cane drops from my hand.

All thought of saving myself vanishes in the blink of an eye.

I watch it fall, twirling end over end like a baton through the air. It falls into a huge snow drift, disappearing from sight.

I have no idea if it's broken or not.

But it might as well be.

It's gone, and I'm caught, and Christmas is ruined forever.

8

JOY

I THRASH MINDLESSLY against the demon holding me, but his grip remains firm. Desperation surges through me, turning my blood to molten lava, and I do the only thing I can think of—I bite down on his hand. Hard.

He releases a muffled curse, his grip loosening just enough that I'm able to wiggle my body free...apparently forgetting that I'm miles and miles above the ground.

"Oh shit!" I manage to stutter out as the demon's grin turns malicious and cruel. With a wink that sends chills shooting through me like fallen stars, he releases me completely, and I drop.

Air rushes past my ears as I begin to freefall towards the ground below.

I don't want to die! That one thought plays on repeat in my head as I somersault through the air, my dress whipping around me and my apron flipping over my face, obscuring my vision.

Fear bombards me, the sheer intensity like a knife to my gut, as I see the ground rush up to greet me. I think of my father, wherever he may be. Trapped. Hurt. Broken. Completely at the mercy of the sadistic demons currently ruling the North Pole. I think of the innocent cherubs, caught in a battle they can never hope to win.

And then, surprisingly enough, I think of my reindeer. Who will feed them cookies? Though the cherubs are kind and pure, they're too lazy to make all of the reindeer special treats. I suppose my pets will have to eat oats and carrots for the rest of their time like the rest of the animals. Will they miss me?

But the second my body would've made contact with the ground, the second I would've become a Joy-shaped pancake, a furry body swoops in and veers skywards. I release a pained "oomf" as I land on Donner's back, the two of us rising towards the sky. For a brief moment, the wind is knocked out of me and I struggle to breathe. My breaths saw in and out as I orient myself on Donner, gripping his neck with a grip like an iron vise.

In the distance, I can see the shadowy silhouettes of the rest of my reindeer hurrying towards us, and the relief I feel is instantaneous. They're alive, and though they appear bloody and battered—Blitzen has a particularly nasty gash over his right eye, and Comet's antlers are covered in blood, though now that I'm thinking about it, I doubt the blood is his—they're all in relatively one piece.

I'm in one piece.

"Donner, you saved me!" I don't know if my words are able to carry over the roaring of the wind, but I'm pretty sure he makes a strange sound of acknowledgment, something between a chirp and a grunt.

As we continue to fly, the buildings getting smaller and smaller until they're nothing but mushroomed-shaped, red and green colored roofs poking through the boughs of snowy trees, my body relaxes incrementally. I find myself sagging forward, resting my cheek on the back of Donner's fuzzy head, between his antlers. He makes another low noise in the back of his throat, and this time, I almost think it's a purr. Can reindeer purr?

But that mundane thought is soon swept away by a tidal wave of guilt and self-loathing.

I lost the cane.

I found all of the ingredients and reassembled it, only to drop it into a huge snow drift seconds later. I couldn't even give the damn thing to Santa before my clumsy ass ruined it.

Tears of indignation prick my eyes, but I refuse to let them fall. There'll be a time for that later, but for now, we need to get somewhere safe. The reindeer aren't capable of staying in the air forever, and I can already see Blitzen lagging behind, both because of his injury and his natural affinity for sleep.

My eyes scan the snowy landscape before me, currently shrouded in a fine layer of wispy snow, before they hook on a tiny cabin located in a thicket of trees.

"There!" I point towards the minuscule structure as Donner twists his body in that direction, the rest of the reindeer following him.

As we get closer, I can see that the building is nothing more than a single-room cabin made of roughly hewn logs. Both of the windows are dirty, as if the owner hasn't bothered to clean them in a while, and long, spindly, red and green weeds poke through the snow along the curving driveway. Last I heard, the owner of this house left a few years ago, after...

Donner slows to a stop, and Cupid reaches my side, nudging my hand with a question in his eyes.

"My ex-boyfriend, Zacharia, used to live here," I explain as I slide off of Donner and walk on shaky legs to the entrance. He was an angel interning with Santa, hoping to take over for my dad when he hit retirement age. He was given this cabin as a way to stay away from the politics that accompany the North Pole and Christmas Village. Of course, my dad didn't realize that I used to sneak away to fuck Zacharia senseless. When I broke up with him, he was devastated, but I knew a relationship between the two of us would never last. He had a Center somewhere out there, and until he found her—or him—he would never be truly happy.

Cupid gives me a droll look, almost as if he's pissed at me for taking him to a place I used to fuck a guy, and Dasher goes as far as to stick his antlers through one of the windows, shattering the glass and then turning towards me with innocent, Bambi eyes. Fuckers. I'm pretty sure Comet is peeing on one of the sugar plum bushes, just to make a statement. Sometimes, I swear these reindeer are sentient beings who can actually understand what I'm saying to them. It wouldn't surprise me. There are far weirder things in both Heaven and Hell, creepy demon children included.

The front door is unlocked—no one would dare to try to steal anything in the North Pole—and I quickly flick on all of the light switches, illuminating the cabin in a musty, golden glow. It's exactly as I remember it, with a single table in the far corner surrounded by two chairs, and a kitchen that is larger than even the living room. A bathroom is against the far wall—there's not even a door to separate it from the living room, because angels don't believe in privacy—and the bedroom itself is in a loft above us. It's small, but it'll be safe and warm for the night until we can come up with a Plan B. And C. And D, E, F, and G. Hell, let's just come up with an entire alphabet this time, because knowing my piss-poor luck, I'll screw it up. Again.

A wave of sheer fury and frustration explodes inside of me, and before I realize what I'm doing, I'm slamming my fist into the window that Dasher didn't break. Glass embeds itself into my knuckles, pain reverberating across my hand, but it's nothing compared to the pain in my chest, steadily choking my airways until it feels as if I can't breathe.

"Fuck!" I scream, preparing to throw another punch at the window, but before I can make contact, Cupid is in front of me, his dark head canted to the side. I could be mistaken, I usually am, but his eyes almost appear… sad. Heartbreakingly sad, as if I had shoved my fist into his chest instead of a window.

And that expression…

It shatters me.

I feel like one of those ugly Christmas sweaters that humans love to wear that, overtime, has become riddled with holes. The thread is unraveling, and the slightest tug will destroy it completely. I'm that sweater, and this moment is that damn thread being tugged within an inch of its pathetic life.

I failed Santa.

I failed Christmas.

I failed myself.

Tears drip down my cheeks as I collapse on the floor, cradling my injured hand to my chest. Immediately, all of the reindeer gather around me, nuzzling and licking me. I reach for the nearest reindeer, Dasher, and bury my face in his neck. My hands loop around Comet's body on the other side of me as I tug him closer. Cupid and Blitzen both place their heads in my lap, while Donner whines and nibbles on the strands of my blonde hair.

As my tears settle on their fur, seeping into their skin, I'm suddenly aware of a tingling sensation dancing across my arms. I pull my head away from Donner's mouth and slowly remove my hands from Comet, staring at the shaky limbs in disbelief.

What the hell?

In the blink of an eye, a blinding white light consumes my vision, splattered with dark spots like a paintbrush tossing paint haphazardly on a canvas. I attempt to shield myself from the brilliant glow, believing that the demons have come to attack us again, but I feel no pain.

Gradually, the light recedes, and the cabin is once more submerged in the familiar murky, golden sheen from the hanging bulb.

I blink rapidly, my hands automatically reaching for my reindeer.

But instead of soft fur, my hands connect with…human flesh.

My eyes snap open completely as I stare at the five sinfully gorgeous men surrounding me. All of them are beautiful in their own way.

The man to the side of me, where my head was buried in Dasher's fur, has thick black hair that makes the harsh angles of his face appear cruel and hard. Or that could be the scowl marring his thick lips.

And the two men in my lap…

One of them has sandy-blond hair and is blinking just as quickly as I was a few seconds ago, almost as if he needs glasses to see. The other one has light brown hair that hangs in shaggy waves to his shoulders, like he couldn't be bothered to trim it.

Cupid and Blitzen.

To the left of me is the prettiest man I have ever seen with golden hair streaked with lighter honey-tones. His skin is blemish-free, a literal work of art, and accentuates his abnormally high cheekbones and thin, aristocratic lips, currently pulled into an impish smirk. Is that handsome man Comet?

I tilt my head upwards, the movement almost mechanical, to stare at the last man.

This one has a mane of thick red hair and an unruly beard that makes him look more rugged than the others. More feral. His eyes flash mischievously as his long, nimble fingers pull at my hair. Donner?

And then all at once, the five of them freeze.

Slowly, with the same shock and awe that I just displayed, they stare down at their human bodies. Their *naked* bodies.

"Ya guys seeing this?" the red-haired man behind me demands, his voice thick with a Scottish accent.

"I'm a real boy!" the gorgeous one practically squeals, immediately reaching down to grip his half-hard cock. His eyes roll into the back of his head. "Baby, I missed you so much."

"What...?" My voice is too quiet for them to hear, a low whisper that gets carried away by the frigid wind barreling through the broken windows.

"How is this possible?" the one who appears as if he needs glasses queries, moving his head off my lap. My eyes automatically latch onto his thick cock, before I force my gaze upwards, shock momentarily stealing coherent thoughts.

What the fuck is happening? And where are my reindeer? Who are these men?

"Magic," the long-haired one says, shaking his shaggy head from side to side. His eyelids droop, almost as if he's fighting off sleep, just like Blitzen always used to do. "It has to be."

"What?" My voice is louder this time, a shrill screech, and all at once, I have the attention of all five men in the room. And that's when I notice.

The beautiful blond haired one…he has *horns*. Golden horns that poke through his golden hair.

And the man beside me, with hair as dark as pitch, he has *wings*. Spindly, bat-like wings with ruby red veins crawling up the interior.

No. No. No.

I'm surrounded by demons.

In a tiny recess of my brain, I know that these demons were once my reindeer…my best friends. But I can barely focus on that over the pounding of my heart. *Thump. Thump. Thump. Thump.*

Maybe I was wrong. Maybe the biggest threat isn't the demons currently residing in Christmas Village.

Maybe the biggest threat is right here in this room, surrounding me.

Because if there are a bunch of demons here...

Then I know I'm seconds away from being killed.

9

BRYN, AKA BLITZEN

Joy BOLTS out of the cabin, her hand still bleeding. I was half asleep, but the fact that our mate literally just dashed out the door into freezing weather to escape us, blasting us all with arctic air when she yanked the door open, has left me wide awake.

That, and the fact that we're finally demons again.

How the how? What the what? I stare down at my own hands and just marvel at the fact that I have a thumb again. I won't have to pick up every damned thing with my mouth. That right there is a miracle.

Cupid—I mean Cal, our leader, says, "We've got to find clothes and go after Joy!" He squints around the room, unable to "see" without glasses—I say that sarcastically.

His vision is perfectly fine, but he's a wee bit dramatic —and stomps over to the bathroom to look for something.

Of course he does. He doesn't even need a minute to process what's going on. Cal's all action.

"How are we gonna explain this?" Nico gestures up and down at himself, his huge Highlander body like something out of some middle-aged woman's Scottish porn book collection

"I don't fucking know yet, but we're going to find a way."

"You're off your head!" Nico runs a hand through his red locks. "How are we going to explain that we wanted to do the exact same thing as those other blokes, but we failed? How's she ever going to trust us?"

"She will! Don't worry about it! She's our mate, and she needs our help!" Cal yells as I hear him yank on a shower curtain, a series of *pings* sounding as all the shower rings fall to the tile floor.

None of us can argue with that.

Joy does need us.

As a sloth demon, I'm not the ideal guy. I'm not really the proactive type. But even I know that our sweet Center has bitten off more than she can chew. My mother's recommendation when you take too big a bite is just to spit it back out on the plate and eat it later. Pure sloth demon brilliance right there. But I'm not sure Joy will have much later if she keeps letting those other demon assholes run Christmas Village into the ground. They seem intent on destroying Christmas, which seems like a bit too much work, in my opinion. It's better just to warp it a bit. Make it a smidge disappointing. That sort of thing. Gradually let people down until they don't care any longer. Sloth demons have been doing it for centuries. It's a tried and true technique. It works. But I didn't see a sloth demon amongst that other murder. Idiots. They're going to try to shove change through all at once. That never works.

Sin is a gradual process.

I glance around the room, looking for something I can wear. It's pretty fricking bare, and, no surprise, the other demons have claimed whatever could be taken already.

Comet—no, Dem has stolen the tablecloth right off the table and has it on like a toga. "Last one outside is a rotten angel!" he says as he darts to the front door. He's gone in a flash.

Dasher—dammit, my brain has become used to thinking of the guys as reindeer, and I'm forgetting their real names—Gus runs a tattooed hand through his dark hair and worries his lip piercing before setting his gaze on the couch. He lets his claws extend and rips right through an ancient couch cushion, shredding the edges and using the ragged square of cloth in the middle to make some kind of loincloth for himself.

"Pure dead brilliant," Nico says, grabbing another cushion and attempting to do the same. The frustration demon is a little more patient with his cushion than Gus was, and his square comes out bigger and better. "Almost like a kilt." He shreds the underside of his cushion and ties the two squares together to cover himself before flying out the door too.

Gus's wrath demon nature works against him, and he ends up with basically a man thong. "Fuck it," he says, once he has it on. He's gone a second later.

Cal comes out then, a shower curtain tied around his waist like a skirt. Apparently, he found some glasses in the bathroom too, because there's an old pair with thick frames perched on his nose. "Where the hell is everybody?"

"They left," I shrug.

He glances down at me. "Well, find something to wear, and come on!" Then he leaves too.

I sigh. Shredding the couch seems like too much work, and all the other good, easy options are gone. I suppose I could see if there's a sheet…but the bedroom's so far away. I glance down and notice a bit of gray fabric tucked under the edge of the couch. I bend down and yank on it. A balled-up, old sock comes out.

I stare at it a second, and then at the strips of cloth that Gus left behind. "Perfect." I tuck my junk into the old sock and use one of the pre-made couch strips to tie around my waist to hold it on. Then I fight off a yawn as I walk to the door and head out into the cold to go find Joy.

Only my mate could make me work so fricking hard.

But I think of Joy's cookies and her smile and launch myself into the air. Come hell or high water, I'm gonna make that beautiful girl smile again. Right after I convince her that we aren't working with those other guys.

WHEN I LAND NEXT TO THE OTHER GUYS, THEY'VE GOT Joy surrounded in a copse of evergreens that are taller than three Christmas stables stacked on top of one another. The snow packed underneath them is still three feet or so tall, because everywhere in this Christmas realm is covered in snow. It's incredibly annoying when one wants to nap.

But I don't notice the snow as much as my mate right now. She's trembling. In fear. Tears shine in her eyes.

"Joy!" I call out softly as I land. *Shit! Why is our mate frightened?*

Then I realize that Gus is pacing, his tattooed fingers clenching and unclenching. *Dammit. Did the wrath demon scare her?* Gus tends to fly off the handle when he's agitated. And I'm pretty sure the body swap we just did counts as a major disruption to the wrath demon.

We don't even know what caused it. I mean...damn, if we knew how to change back, we would have done it years ago. Who knows how long it will even last? I shut off that worried train of thought and focus on Gus. And his idiocy. He made our Joy cry.

I'm not usually one for brawls, I prefer bubble baths, but I wind up and clock him. Gus is so shocked that he falls straight backwards into the snow.

"What the fuck?" he says, gripping his chin where I hit him. He doesn't get out of the snow though, doesn't attack me back. I have to assume it's from the shock that a sloth demon just trounced him.

"Do. Not. Make. Joy. Scared!" I tell him with a firm point of my finger.

"Dude, I didn't do it! Dem got here first! He made her cry!"

"What the fuck, Dem?" I whirl towards him, lit up with a fury that I've never felt before. Most of my feelings are muted by an overwhelming need to sleep. Not today, apparently. Not when it comes to Joy. I glare at the thievery demon with everything I've got.

"I just tried to steal a kiss!" Dem tosses his hands up like he's innocent.

WHAM.

Another hit, and another member of my murder plops into the snow. The pretty boy is gonna have one hell of a shiner. I'm on fire.

"Anybody else here terrorizing my mate?" I ask through my teeth, fists clenched and raised in front of me in preparation. I half want to dance on the balls of my feet like some pro fighter in a ring, but that requires too much energy.

Cal shakes his head. "No, man."

I'm not sure I believe him. He *is* a white lie demon.

"Mate? What?" Joy's voice is breathless. I turn to look at her, her golden locks spilling down her shoulders, her eyes wide. Those lips… My eyes are instantly drawn to the plush line of her lips. I've felt them on the top of my head before, but never against mine. I wonder for a second what it would feel like to brush her lips against my own. But she's not ready for that. Not yet. I'm not like Dem, who can steal kisses. No, I'll wait until she's ready—ready for me, for all of us.

125

My eyes slowly rise to meet hers. "You're our Center, Joy. We've been trapped as reindeer for years. And we're all desperately in love with you."

"I was about to say that." Cal swats at me. He doesn't like his leadership upstaged.

"Liar," I say, calling him out. Because Cal will dance around the truth if he gets half a chance. It's just in his nature.

But our mate deserves the truth, even if it terrifies her. Even if she runs in the opposite direction, choosing to face the demons alone rather than deal with five men she doesn't know confessing their love for her.

"We want to help you," I tell her, resisting the urge to take her hands. The need to touch her is like an itch, one I have to resist scratching.

I've always felt the need to be around her, but now that I'm in my normal form, that need has been multiplied by a hundred. The need to cuddle her, to have her fall asleep in my arms, the need to lazily wake up and gaze into her sleepy, contented eyes... Images flash through my mind and fill me with longing.

I've never been one for casual touch, but apparently, my mate turns me into a big old teddy bear. Who would've thought?

But I'll only ever get to make those fantasies a reality if we help her rout out these assholes who've tried to steal her home.

"Joy, we want to help you, but give me a minute with these assholes, because they clearly don't know how to treat a lady."

I grab Cal by the arm, and I narrow my eyes at Nico, daring him to defy me. I see him lick his lips and clench his hands—the temptation is strong—but the frustration demon doesn't give in to his powers. He follows me, smoothing his makeshift kilt as he does.

So do the two idiots I punched.

Follow me, I mean. Not smooth out their kilts like the glowering Scot.

When we're about ten feet away from Joy, I let my gaze fall onto each one of them in turn. "Joy is our Center. That means we do what she wants. Not what we want. Got it?" I glare at Dem. "No more stealing kisses, no matter how tempting that might be. You wait until the lady asks. And if she doesn't want to kiss you but tells you she wants you to kiss Cal's cock? You do it."

I hear Joy gasp, and Dem makes a face of distaste. We may not be attracted to each other, but if Joy wants me sucking a ballsack, you can bet your ass I'll be sucking a ballsack. Hopefully, it's the ballsack of one of my fellow demons. The ballsack you know and all that. I'm pretty sure I read that on a Snapple cap.

But I'm serious. These idiots need to understand I mean it. "If you so much as make a tear come to her eye ever again, I will ensure your dick stays so limp and dead that you won't ever be able to orgasm."

That makes every demon's eyes widen.

Because, yeah, erectile dysfunction? Totally an invention of the sloth demons. When we decide to get mean, we get really fucking mean.

"You wouldn't," Cal whispers, shoving his glasses up nervously. But even he doesn't believe his own lie.

I raise a brow. "Try me."

Every single one of them gulps and moves to cup their cocks, as if they can protect their dicks from my sleepy wrath. And I feel a little rush. For a second, I wonder if this is what Gus feels every time he gets into a fight. Maybe. It would explain why he's always so eager for them.

Since I've clearly taken the lead—you should just put a crown on my head and call me the King of Demons. Actually. Don't. That requires too much fucking work —I jerk my head towards our mate. "Now, get over there and convince Joy that we're going to help her save Christmas."

10

JOY

CENTER? Mate?

Obviously, I know what a Center is. I live with angels, for fuck's sake, and every angel flock wishes to find a Center of their own. Apparently, it's a fated mate and the only thing in all of the universes that can make a group of either angels or demons vulnerable.

And to hear that these demons think that I'm their Center...

It's ridiculous. They're lying. There is no way in hell that I'm the Center to a bunch of demons attempting to destroy my home and family. Anger momentarily darkens my vision at the thought that these men could be using me, but I shove that emotion beneath the proverbial rug. I need to be smart about how I play this. Either they're pretending that I'm their Center to lure me into a false sense of security and comfort, or...

Or they truly believe that I'm their Center. And if that's the case, then I may be able to use that to my advantage.

The tears dry up as quickly as they arrive, and I straighten my spine almost imperceptibly as the demons return from their huddle. My lips twitch before I can stop them, because for a moment, they looked like one of those human sports teams attempting to make a gameplay. You know the one... with the tight pants that make their asses look amazing. I may have become a huge American football fan because of that. And I also may have banged a few players, because *hello.* Tight pants, chiseled asses, and abs begging to be licked? That's any human's wet dream, even a half-human like me.

"Joy," one of the demons begins in a placating manner, taking a few steps closer until he's directly in front of me. I try to stand my ground, try to keep my chin up, but I wobble backwards a few steps until my back is against one of the potently-smelling pine trees.

His face falls, but he stops a few paces in front of me. I can't help but notice that he appears to be the leader of this ragtag group, with sandy-blond hair that frames an angelically beautiful face. Glasses—he must've found a pair of them inside of the cabin—slip down his nose as he tilts his head to the side and stares at me. The intensity of his gaze is unnerving, and goosebumps skitter up my spine.

"Don't…" I warn, my voice shaking slightly. I don't know what I'm warning him against, but either way, his expression shutters even more.

"My name is Cal," the demon continues, his middle finger lifting to push his glasses back up his nose. "And I'm a white lie demon."

"White lie demon?" I wrap my arms around my stomach. "What does that mean?"

"It means you never hear an honest word out of that fool's mouth…except for when he's talking to you, apparently," the largest man responds in a lilting accent. He has the reddest hair I've ever seen, cascading to his shoulders like fire. His eyes glimmer mischievously as Cal's own gaze hardens.

"Nico…" Cal warns the large man, but Nico simply throws his head back in laughter before turning towards me. I swear his expression softens, and the lazy demon's words from before replay in my head.

"We're all desperately in love with you."

Is that true?

Do they…

Do they love me?

My head is beginning to pound as confusion and something akin to hope war for dominance. I smother each of the emotions before they can consume me entirely.

They *can't* love me. They barely know me. At least, I barely know them…though I don't know what that has to do with them loving me.

You can't even think coherently anymore, Joy, a snarky voice hisses in my head.

"Nico." The redheaded Scot extends a hand, heat flaring in his eyes when I take it in my own. His is so much larger than mine, his palm calloused and riddled with scars from when he was a reindeer. "But you probably know me as Donner."

It makes sense why he can scar, I think to myself unwittingly. *If I'm truly his Center, those scars would be because of his close proximity to me.*

But I'm not. His Center, that is.

My heart hammers in my chest, threatening to escape at any moment, but fear keeps it adequately subdued. Until I figure out if these demons are friends or foes, I need to be on guard. I can't allow them to sneak past my defenses. That would be the prime time to stick a knife in my back.

"I'm Dem." This comes from the prettiest man of the bunch. I never thought I would refer to a man as pretty, but that's what he is. He's fucking gorgeous, a literal angelic work of art that people would tithe to. "The most famous reindeer of all. Comet."

"Comet," I repeat slowly, my eyes traveling across his perfectly symmetric face to his pale golden hair to his cerulean blue eyes, the color brighter than any I've ever seen before. My gaze lingers on his chest—bronze skin pulled taut over slender muscle—before I force it away. "You're the one who always steals my cookies."

"And your panties," Nico adds helpfully, and I swear, the pretty boy demon blushes.

"I'm a thievery demon," he confesses. "I can't help it. I need to steal like Bryn over there needs to sleep."

I turn towards the second to last demon, still surprised that the sleepy demon or whatever is the man who just took charge a few minutes earlier. Only now, his eyelids are droopy, and I'm pretty sure he's sleeping standing up. His head lolls against his chest, his shaggy brown hair obscuring his features from view. Unlike the others, he only has a sock covering his…um…*thing* from view. And it's *barely* covering. There's no doubt that Bryn is packing some massive heat.

"Bryn!" Cal snaps, stalking towards the demon and shoving his shoulder. Bryn's eyes fly open, and he twists in both directions, as if searching for a threat that doesn't exist. When he turns his back to me, I'm able to see his chiseled ass, and oh mylanta. I may be wary of the demons, but that ass will fuel my spank bank for years to come. Centuries to come, assuming I don't die in this fucked up mess.

"Youwanname?" Bryn mumbles, releasing a yawn so huge that his mouth takes up half of his face. For some reason, that doesn't deter from his raw sex appeal.

"I have no idea what you just said," Cal snaps, before shooting me an apologetic look. He once again pushes his glasses up his nose, and I'm beginning to believe that's a nervous habit of his. Do demons even need glasses?

"Sorry," Bryn murmurs, yawning again. He faces me, and some of the sleepiness seems to fade from his face like a curtain being drawn open. "I'm Brynjarr. Bryn. Blitzen." He waves a hand in the air dismissively, almost as if he already said too much and now his throat hurts from talking. Still, he manages to yawn out, "Sloth demon."

Finally, I turn to the last demon. The scariest. With his dark hair, tattoos, and numerous piercings, he's a sight to behold. And don't even get me started on the rage emanating from his nearly black eyes. I don't know what type of demon he is, but he looks as if he wants to murder everyone in this entire planet, including me.

Well, maybe excluding me, if the heat that springs to life is any indication. Still, unease trickles down my back as he pierces me with a stare capable of turning milk into butter. Intermixed with my unease is a lust so strong and potent, it nearly takes my breath away.

A twisted, demented part of me wants to take the brunt of his anger. Wants to feel his hands around my throat as his cock destroys my pussy. Wants his fingers to leave bruises on my skin while my own nails create trails on his back.

What is happening to me?

I've never felt lust on such a visceral level, and the intensity of the emotion confuses me. I feel lust for all five of the demons, even knowing that they're here to hurt me and my father. That they want to take over the North Pole.

Or…

Do they?

"The broody fellow is Zorgos, or Gus. Wrath demon," Nico says, pointing towards tall, dark, and sexy. "Dasher was his reindeer name."

"Shut the fuck up!" Gus bellows, and the sheer intensity and suddenness of his rage sends me staggering back a couple of steps. "I can speak for myself!"

I can physically see him trying to regain control of his turbulent emotions. His breaths saw in and out as he takes a deep, calming breath. And then, his dark eyes lock on mine.

The change is instantaneous. One second, he looks as if he's the Grim Reaper himself, come to take Nico's soul straight to Hell, and the next, he looks serene, the harsh planes of his face smoothing over.

It's almost as if I soothed him. Tamed him. Which is ridiculous, because there's no way I'm their Center.

Maybe if I tell myself that enough times, I'll begin to believe it.

"As Bryn said—" Before Cal can finish speaking, Gus jabs him in the stomach with his elbow and pushes him out of the way.

"Maybe the lying demon shouldn't be in charge of explanations," he states dryly, moving to stand in front of me and consuming my entire vision. This close, I can see a piercing in his lower lip and another in his eyebrow. His hair is the darkest color I've ever seen before, almost appearing blue in the waning sunlight. With snow landing on his shoulders, he's too achingly beautiful for me to even look at. That's what his beauty reminds me of—pain. He's physically *painful* to be around, because his beauty is almost ethereal. Harsh and masculine and raw.

"Tell me the truth," I whisper stubbornly, tilting my chin up. He's so damn tall that I'm pretty sure I break my neck in my attempt to maintain eye contact. "Why are you here?"

"Why we came is different than why we stayed." His voice is practically a growl, but this time, I don't feel any fear. I almost feel…protected. Safe. Cared for. Which is ridiculous.

Right?

"Tell me the truth," I repeat.

"We came to enjoy the candy canes," Cal pipes in, nervously fiddling with his glasses once more. Up the bridge of his nose. Then back down. Then up again. Then back down.

"Lie," Nico hollers with a raspy laugh and a toss of his red hair. To me, he confesses, "We came to steal Christmas, just like those other bastards are doing." Anger leaks through his words as he crosses his arms over his broad chest. "But your daddy caught us and turned us into reindeer."

"And now?" I can practically feel my heart breaking, shredding into thousands of pieces smaller than the glitter the cherubs throw into the boxes of kids whose parents are on the naughty list. If they tell me that they're here to help the other demons, destroy my home and family…

You don't know them, Joy. Not really. You knew the reindeer they were pretending to be, not the demons they actually are. Don't go getting hurt feelings now.

But that motto is easier to say in my head than apply in real life. All I can think about is the way Blitzen used to cuddle beside me whenever I visited him at the barn, his sleepy eyes blinking up at me as he tried to stay awake. The way Comet would always steal the last cookie. And my socks. And my shoes. And my coat. The way Donner would annoy his brothers by pouncing on them and headbutting them and being a real pain in their asses. Dasher's growly but protective presence, always following me around whenever I was on a date and attempting to pierce the guy with his horns. And then Cupid, who kept the others in line and always looked at me with eyes that made me feel invincible and loved. I thought they were my pets, the best pets I ever fucking had, but they've always been so much more.

"Why are you here?" I say for the third time, waiting with bated breath for their answer.

For once, I detect no deceit in Cal's words when he speaks next. He's being one hundred percent truthful, going against his baser nature to answer me. "We're here for you, Joy. We've always been here for you."

11

GUS, AKA DASHER

I FIDDLE with my lip ring while Joy decides whether or not she's going to trust us. If she doesn't, I swear I'm gonna punch Cal so hard, he blacks out. I crack my knuckles in anticipation, feeling the heat of anger travel up my spine.

Until Joy smiles.

Fuck. All that heat transforms into something else. Instead of zigzagging through me like lightning, it blooms like a fucking rose on my dick. I mean, my dick gets hot and hard as fuck. Not sure where that flowery bullshit came from.

Goddammit. Being a stupid deer has bashed in my masculinity-meter a bit. Maybe I need to punch something to get it back. Bryn is nearly asleep again. He'd make a good target.

Joy clears her throat, and once again, my power abandons me, just sluices away like an iceberg breaking off from a glacier.

What the hell did Santa's spell do to me? Fuck. Maybe it's all those years of listening to him read poetry aloud in the barn. I thought it was to torture us at the time... and now it seems like I've internalized that crap.

I don't have more than a second to blast red-hot angry thoughts in Santa's direction before Joy speaks with the voice of an angel.

That one's not poetry. She's literally a half-angel. Shut up.

"If you're here for me, prove it," she states, trying to keep the waver out of her voice, but I can tell the bravado camouflages her fear. After centuries with Cal, one can tell a lie from a truth with a bit more accuracy than before.

"Happy to prove it, pretty girl," I tell her. "Want me to break their bones until they quake with regret? Want me hook my claws in their eyeballs and pop them out—"

Joy gags, so I stop.

"Too much?" I ask. My wrath knows no bounds.

"Too much," she nods. "How about we just kick them out?" She bites her lip, uncertain. Of course, Santa's daughter would be worried that even kicking out demons was too much. Surrounded by all this goody two shoes bullcrap twenty-four-seven, it's a miracle that my little Center is as much of a rebel as she is.

"Yeah, we can totally do that," Cal lies. "We'll just kick them out. Nothing else." Sometimes, Cal's lies are pretty damn convenient. He slides his arm around our soulmate and says, "I'm sure we can call them over and have a nice discussion about it, work it all out…"

Joy shrugs out from beneath his arm, her lush green eyes narrowing in suspicion. "Talk it out?"

"Yeah, you know, wave the white flag, have a temporary ceasefire. Don't worry. I'll take care of all the details, cookie," he says, tossing out the nickname nonchalantly.

"Cal, you're lying." Joy crosses her arms, frustration marring that beautiful face of hers.

Yeah, he's lying. Demons don't adhere to ceasefire bullshit. They're like bombs, set to commence destruction within a certain time frame no matter where they land.

I look to Nico for help, since there's no way I'll be able to join this conversation without at least giving Cal a black eye for lying to our girl.

Luckily, the Scot steps up to the plate. He pats down his makeshift kilt as he says, "Excuse the bampot, lovie. He's thick-headed sometimes. We can just annoy the shit out of that murder and convince them Christmas isn't worth it. We can put ice in their sheets, so they climb into a wet, cold bed. We can reprogram the dolls to talk in the middle of the night. We can make sure reindeer shit gets in all their damned food. Remember the time we gave some to Cal and told him it was chocolate from Joy?" He can't stop a chuckle from escaping. "Nothing tastes worse than reindeer shit."

Joy puts her hands into her hair in frustration. I don't think Nico's plan is at all what our mate had in mind. She does like some juvenile pranks, but I'm pretty sure, given the number of tears she's shed over this situation, that our Joy is on the edge of despair, and her despair is currently laced with frustration.

I don't like the way her frustration erupts in her little snort of disapproval and then permeates the air around us, making me feel as if we're failing her. I don't want to fail her. I can't. I won't.

The memory of the time she fixed my broken leg, the year the sleigh smashed into it and I had to fly back home with pain and wrath mixing together inside my body, replays in my head. I'd nearly collapsed when we finally got to the Christmas realm. The other reindeer had to basically lug my unconscious ass through the sky to the stable, and only Santa's magic had kept me from being dragged through the snow and run over by his sleigh.

Joy had run out to see her father, but as soon as she'd realized I was hurt, she'd beelined for me instead. I remember that distinctly, blinking snow out of my eyes and seeing her kneel down in front of me, distress etched across her face.

Joy slept with me in my stall that first night, until Santa agreed to let me move into her kitchen for my recovery. Even then, she'd brought down her big red and green quilt and curled up next to me, resting her soft head on my side.

I'd hardly gotten any sleep, just craned my neck so I could stare at her. I'd drug out that recovery for as long as I possibly could, faking a limp even, so that Joy would give me extra cookies and extra pets.

I think I was in love with her even then. Even before I really understood what love was.

I hadn't known for certain she was my Center then, but I'd treasured her above all others. Now that I know what she is, her ire tinged with sadness is too potent for me to stand. I have to do something about it.

I try to shove aside my power for a second and think clearly. "What if we just imprison them? What if we catch and restrain and bind them somehow?"

Joy claps her hands together and leaves them in a prayer position as she points at me. "That. Yes! Let's do that! If we get them locked up, Dad can handle them. We really just need to free him."

I love the way her eyes shimmer when she looks at me, as though a bowl of sugar has tipped over and the sweet sparkles are coating me in—I swear I'm gonna punch myself in the face if this poetry bullshit keeps up.

I take a step closer to Joy, despite the fact that she turns my brain into an emo punk writing crappy love songs in the margins of his notebook during class. I can't help it. That smile calls to me—

I'm smug when I cut that thought off before I can think something ridiculous. A smile even curves my lips upwards, which is rare for a wrath demon.

Joy's intake of breath isn't subtle. Neither is the way her eyes dilate as we stare at each other. I want to grab her so badly, it fucking hurts. But I'm not going to touch her until I've proven myself to her. Proven that all these years, I've been in love with her, whether either of us knew it or not.

I need her to give us a shot.

And I'm going to earn it.

I let my eyes burn into hers as I promise, "We'll do whatever it takes."

She swallows hard and gives a single nod.

Yes.

That one little gesture of approval has my heart doing the tango, a rumba…no. No, my heart is not fucking dancing and flicking its wrist. It's a fucking monster truck, roaring through the air and landing with a satisfying smash on a bunch of cars in a delicious crunch of glass and creak of metal.

There. If I have to spout fucking bullshit, at least it should be as violent as I am.

I turn away from Joy before I wax all poetic again and let my wings stretch. Damn. That feels good. It's been far too long since I got to fly using my own power and not ridiculous Christmas magic.

"Let's do this, fuckers!" I shout.

"Yeah!" Even Bryn responds with a fist pump.

"Um, Gus?" Joy's tentative voice immediately makes me spin around. She bites her lip and gestures at her back. "I don't have—"

She doesn't even finish her sentence before I scoop her into my arms and revel at the feel of her skin touching mine. Her fingers wrap around the back of my neck, her breasts pressing against my chest. I shoot us up into the sky before the moment gets to be too much— and before the other demons try to steal her from me— and I accidentally embarrass myself by calling her eyes liquid pools aloud.

I just embrace the fact that my mate is in my arms, trusting me to rescue her realm, and giving me the green light to fuck some demons up in the process.

Okay, that's a stretch, but roll with me. It's more of a yellow light, and we all know yellow means go faster and don't get caught.

Life doesn't get better than that.

ONCE WE'RE IN FLIGHT, WE COME UP WITH A ROUGH plan. Or Cal does anyway. I'm better at just acting on my anger, improvising.

"Gus, you turn your wrath outwards. Blast them with it so they can't even see straight."

I nod along. I'll try it, at least. With Joy in my arms, I'm a bit more reluctant than usual to join the fight. That was something I didn't think about when I scooped her up into my arms. But really, what demon could resist?

Calvus snaps a finger. "Gus, pay attention! Now, once you blast them, we'll let pretty boy do his thing. Dem, you steal whatever you can find from them while they're blinded with rage. Weapons. Hell, steal their boots so they have to walk barefoot in the snow, I don't care. But disarm them."

Dem gives a confident nod, his wings stretched out flat as he rides a jet stream. "Can do."

Nico pipes up then. He always does. The frustration demon knows it irks Cal when he's interrupted, and the former Scot can't resist. "And then you'll let me tie them together with garlands right? Shove a bit of ginger root up their arses?"

"Ah!" Joy cringes in my arms. "Ginger?"

Nico waves a hand. "You're right, Joy. Some of them might get off on that. Never mind. I'll Gorilla glue their dicks to their thighs. Even better. You're a genius, lovie!"

Joy shares a wide-eyed, disbelieving look of amusement with me. "I'm a genius," she whispers.

My heart fucking soars like Icarus wearing his wax wings and looping too near the sun, not caring that the flight might be the death of me, not caring about the next second, the drip of wax that will spell my doom, not caring about anything but this very moment where I feel weightless.

Joy and I. I and Joy. We. Share. A. Moment.

And I'm so utterly caught up in it that I don't even notice till afterwards that my mind was writing sonnets to her.

Anything. I will do anything for this woman.

That includes flying directly into a thick snow storm that's just started up. We wheel through the air, underneath dark grey clouds that cast a shadow over a realm that's usually merry and bright. It's almost as if the sky itself is crying for Santa and the cherubs, for the Christmas joy that is being devoured by the demons. I tug Joy closer to my chest, sharing my body heat with her and simultaneously trying to shield her from the snow as we move towards Santa's Workshop, which is currently sporting a giant hole in the roof.

Here we go. "We're gonna rock around their Christmas tree!" I declare.

Joy gives me a confused look.

Nico, because he's an asshole, calls out, "You gonna blow them or something?"

Fuck. "That came out wrong."

Joy grins. "No worries. Let me try. We're gonna jingle their bells!"

"Oh no you will not!" Dem growls. "You don't jingle any bells but ours."

Damn right she won't.

Bryn yawns. "How about we're just gonna par-rum-pa-pum-pum… Never mind."

Christmas sayings weren't meant to be badass apparently.

We're going to find some demons and fuck them up.

12

JOY

Gus lands silently behind a large snow bank, just at the edge of the workshop. From this angle, we're able to see through the windows, and horror immediately fills me at the carnage the demons have already caused.

In the far corner of the room, some of our best cherubs are tied up in a cluster. A few of the more mouthy ones are hanging from the ceiling, their faces ashen and eyes wide with terror.

I place a hand over my mouth to stifle my sobs as I stare at my friends' mottled, bruised faces. What did those sick bastards do to them?

"That's fucked up," Gus murmurs, his voice coming from directly beside my ear. I twist my head marginally to meet his piercing stare as silent tears cascade down my blotchy cheeks.

"Would you have done that?" My voice is nothing more than a hushed murmur, barely audible over the roaring wind disrupting the fluffy white snow. When Gus quirks an eyebrow, confusion glimmering in his gaze, I nod towards where the cherubs are huddled, scared shitless and beaten. "Would you have been that cruel?"

Surprisingly, it's not Gus who answers, but Dem, moving to stand on the other side of me. He folds his arms over his chest as his lips curl into a frown. I can tell that he doesn't usually wear that expression. It seems unnatural on his pretty face, as if his facial muscles aren't quite used to making it.

"No," Dem responds, his voice just as quiet as mine. "You have to understand...demons aren't the epitome of evil. At least, not all demons are, just as not all angels are pure and bright and sunny. We represent the dissonant chaos. The disorder in the world and the breaking of societal rules and structure. But we're not..." He makes a face, a muscle in his jaw clenching. "We're not cruel."

"We would've taken over the North Pole, sure," Nico adds, his voice uncharacteristically grave, "but we wouldn't have hurt any of the little fookers. Instead, we would've offered them better benefits than your dad did and get them to work fer us. I mean, does Santa even give them health care?" He shakes his head slowly, red hair bright against the snowy backdrop. "What these demons are doing right now…"

"It's evil," Bryn finishes, yawning heavily. He blinks rapidly at the window as he attempts to stay awake.

"It's only sort of evil," Cal lies as he pushes his glasses up his nose.

"Lie," both Nico and I say dryly.

Cal ignores us and claps his hands together, directing our attention away from the window. "Are you guys ready for this?"

"As ready as we can be," I murmur, my eyes flicking back towards the window and my heart filling with dread. But then…

I see it.

Bangs, the leader of the demon murder, is talking with Blue and Ugly, the three of them laughing while the other two members of their demon squad—including the one who can put us all into a depressive state— terrorize the cherubs. But behind the three of them, resting in the plastic tub of Barbie dolls, is Santa's staff.

It didn't break?!!

"Guys," I whisper, jabbing my elbow into the stomach of the nearest demon. Cal, I realize, when he moves to stand beside me. My hand shakes as I point towards the staff we built, still in one piece and glowing with the red and green tendrils of magic. "If we get that to Santa…" I trail off, but Cal understands immediately where I'm going with it.

If we can get the staff to Santa, this will all be over.

"All right. New plan." He turns briskly around to face the other four, and despite the horrible situation, despite the worry and fear for my friends and father, lust percolates in my stomach before settling in my core. There's something about Cal taking charge that I find immensely and inexplicably sexy. Who am I kidding? There's nothing unexplainable about it. He seems to innately command each of their attention with only a few curt words. And more than that, they follow his directions with decisive head nods.

Cal's a leader, through and through, and if I truly am their Center, which I am finally beginning to believe, then I'm a very lucky girl.

"Gus and Dem, your jobs stay the same. Nico, I want you to cause enough chaos to get the demons away from the staff. Joy and I will steal it while everyone is distracted and fighting."

"And what will I do?" Bryn demands, sounding almost petulant that he hasn't been assigned a specific job…

No wait. He's just half-asleep and struggling to formulate coherent sentences.

Cal's grin sharpens, resembling a shark prowling the ocean for blood.

"Why you, my friend, are going to make all of the demons go nighty night."

IT'S DECIDED. NICO WILL CAUSE A DISTRACTION FIRST. As the demons rush outside, trying to figure out what's going on, Gus will hit them with some mindless wrath to make them vulnerable. That will give Bryn a chance to hit them with his...sleep power? Lazy power? Well, whatever it is, he'll be aiming it at the demons so that Dem can sweep in and steal their weapons while Cal and I take the staff and bring it to Dad.

It's not a surefire plan, but it's better than anything I would've been able to accomplish on my own.

As the guys disperse to move towards their positions, I suddenly find it difficult to breathe. There's a tennis ball-sized lump in my throat, one that makes swallowing impossible.

I grab Dem's arm before he can leave, but like I expected, my sudden movement causes all of them to stop and look at me.

Tears—those damn, wretched things—fill my eyes as I meet each of their stares, allowing my sincerity to emanate from my gaze. Originally, I'd planned to use their attachment to my advantage. But they've been so sincere…minus Cal's lies, which haven't been directed toward me. And suddenly, I find myself feeling attached as well.

"Thank you," I whisper hoarsely. There are a thousand things I'm thanking them for, but I can't articulate what each of them are. For being my friends when they were mere reindeer. For staying with me when they could've left. For helping me now.

For loving me.

"Always, beautiful," Dem says softly, cupping my cheek. His eyes turn molten as they scour my face. "Be careful."

"I will," I assure him, covering his hand with my own. "You be careful too."

His grin widens, revealing those adorable dimples, and he gives me a mock salute with his free hand. "I'm always careful."

"I thought I was the lying demon," Cal deadpans, but Dem simply winks, moving stealthily around the side of the workshop until he disappears from view. His job is the most dangerous. He's got to get closest to the demons in order to swipe their weapons, and anxiety for him rattles my chest like a rain stick turned upside down.

Bryn moves to take his place, and I find myself immediately surrounded by the sloth demon's heat as he pulls me into his arms. He rests his cheek on my head as he rocks us slowly, leisurely, from side to side. I feel comfort in his embrace, my mind immediately conjuring up all of the times I cuddled with Blitzen just like this. He, more than any of my reindeer, liked to place his head in my lap and have me run my fingers through his soft fur, directly between his antlers. I would read him all sorts of stories—everything from *Romeo and Juliet* to *Moby Dick*. Heck, I even threw a few Christmas books in there, enjoying the way his cute little reindeer nose scrunched together in annoyance, before he got too sleepy to give a crap.

"Be safe, Sleepy," I whisper, the stupid nickname leaving my mouth before I can think better of it. Am I really that girl? The type who gives out stupid nicknames? Apparently, I am.

He chuckles, the sound deliciously dark, before pulling away from me.

"Always." He bops my nose before moving to the side, allowing Nico to take his place. The huge Scot doesn't hesitate to take me in his arms and lift me until my feet are a few inches off the ground. He then proceeds to spin me in a wide circle, my blonde hair whipping around my face and my feet accidentally kicking Cal in the hip.

"Ow!" Cal hisses, but Nico merely laughs, placing his mouth to my shoulder to smother the sound.

"Sorry, mate," he says, sounding anything *but* sorry. "You got in the way of my girl's foot." He lowers me to the ground and rests his large hands on my shoulders, his expression turning serious. Tense. A myriad of emotions flickers to life in his vibrant green eyes. "You be safe, you hear me? Because if anything happened to yer…" He squeezes his eyelids shut, almost as if the thought brings him physical pain.

I'm beginning to feel like a broken record when I promise him that I will.

I can only pray that I'm telling them the truth.

Nico and Bryn hurry in the opposite direction Dem went, leaving me alone with Gus and Cal—my wrath and white lie demons.

Gus surprises the shit out of me when he stalks forward, practically shoving Cal out of his way. His hands lift, and he grips my cheeks between his two large, tattooed hands as his dark eyes gleam. And then he kisses me.

His mouth takes mine in a long, lust-filled kiss, one that grows deeper and hungrier with every passing second. His tongue brushes over my lower lip, asking for more, and I'm so shocked by the tentative gesture from the usually demanding demon that I open my mouth for him, giving him *everything*.

Once inside, his tongue plunders my mouth, and his hands grip my face with an intensity that makes me ache.

All too soon, he pulls away from me, both of us panting like we ran a marathon. Ran a marathon…and died halfway through it.

"Fuck," we both breathe at the same time, our eyes locking. I bite my lip to hide my smile as he leans forward and plants one last chaste kiss against my lips in an unspoken promise before he backs away.

"Wish me luck." His dopey smile fades into something grim and *wrathful*. He strides towards the front door of the workshop as if he owns it. As if he owns the fucking world.

"I am not at all turned on right now," Cal says, discreetly adjusting himself.

"Lie," I say with a small smile, one that instantly fades when Nico flies up out of nowhere, a giant red bag in his hands as he wings his way through the air.

I watch Gus yank open the door and stroll inside the workshop like death and vengeance personified. My heart fires off like a missile, hurtling through space. There's no turning back now.

Cal takes my hand and pulls me to the side, just as an enraged bellow reverberates through the still night.

He gives my hand a squeeze, his face grim. "It's time."

13

NICO, AKA DONNER

It's fooking on!

A thrill races up my spine faster than a spider outrunning a shoe. I've got Santa's magical bag on my back packed full of goodies for naughty demons.

I couldn't find coal, but I hurl several nice boulders from the bag down onto the workshop roof. They give a satisfying clang as they dent the metal and then roll off with a groan, before dropping and disappearing into the snowbanks near the walls.

When I'm out of rocks, I snag a Bluetooth speaker that the cherubs keep in the barn and blast some heavy metal. Damn. I cannae say how much I've missed that music stuck here in the land of eternally obnoxious jingles.

There's a good, long scream from the lead singer that reminds me nostalgically of the picnics we used to have next to the murderer's canyon in Hell. It's a beautiful sound, one that is sure to bring any demons in the area looking, wondering what delicious torture is going on.

Seconds later, the other demon group appears. A couple of them are chasing Gus, their eyes lit pure red in fury as they pelt after my brother, the door of the workshop slamming behind them. He weaves between some evergreen trees, and they howl in rage, their sounds mixing perfectly with the angry anthem blaring from my speaker.

I turn when another demon flies up through the hole they made in the workshop roof, his horns glinting in a bit of sun that pops out from behind some clouds. That one shoots towards me like a dart. Unlike the other demons, his eyes aren't bright red. Looks like Gus missed one with his wrath.

I roll to the side, letting the fooker shoot past me and grinning when I hear him growl in annoyance. *That's right, you disgusting hacket of a hellion*, I think. *Come and get me.* I pretend I don't notice him as I reach again into the magical sack, feeling around for my next weapon.

The demon, whose face is as pale as the snow, flies at me with bared teeth like some kind of rabid dog. A saner demon might be put off or intimidated, but me? I love it when I drive others a bit mad. And it's been so verra long since I've been able to do it effectively.

I let him get within spitting distance before I shoot up higher. As soon as he follows, I drop like a stone. Up. Drop. Up. Drop. It's a little game that makes him screech. If he was a dragon shifter, I've no doubt he'd be spitting fire.

I pull my next weapon from Santa's sack, and part of me really wants to shout out "Freedom!" in tribute to Mel Gibson. But I don't. Instead, I sling blue paint through the air so that it douses my enemy, coating him like some sickly afterbirth because the paint chunks up in the cold air and looks like cottage cheese on his skin.

I cannae help it. I laugh uproariously at this. "Oh, you're a sad sight now!"

He divebombs me with a speed I didn't realize he possessed, and my heart fondles my tonsils for a second.

Fook.

That's an unpleasant surprise, to find out he's actually that damn fast. Has he been toying with me? Realization dawns. I wonder if some of these bastards are unpleasant surprise demons. You know, the assholes who make sure your mother unexpectedly fills in as a chaperone at prom, who make you scramble to find a ride to work when your car won't start, the ones who ensure you find a sext message from someone else on your boyfriend's phone. They're right arseholes they are.

I met one or two during my transition from tortured soul to demon. Cannae say it was fun to know them, but that power would explain their ability to sneak up on Santa. If a few demons in that murder have surprise powers and combine them…damn. That will make them harder to fight than the Loch Ness monster. Who cannae be fought because she isn't real.

Santa would just turn around, and bam! His worst nightmare would be in his face. I don't want to find out what unpleasant surprises these demons might have in store for me.

I dive for the workshop, eyes scanning the ground as I feel the demon behind me, his breath heating my neck as his claws rake the back side of my left wing. Where the fook is Bryn? Did he fall asleep on the job?

Stupid sloth demon.

I throw the bag behind me in a desperate attempt to throw this arsehole off course, but other than a muffled *whomp*, I can't be sure it worked. I definitely don't have the time to glance back, not when I feel a claw pierce my wing a bit.

I dive through the hole in the workshop roof, past the cherubs still strapped to the ceiling, ignoring them when they shriek, "No! More demons! We're done for!" Overdramatic whiners.

I head right for my favorite toys in the place. The Nerf guns. I snag one mid-flight and whirl around so I can pelt the fooker behind me with bright yellow balls. They fire through the air and pelt his torso, sticking a bit to the crusty paint before sliding down and getting caught on his pants, gathering around his midsection like pollen grains. With the blue paint… "You look like a fooking flower!" I compliment him.

His hand lifts, and suddenly, my kilt feels like sandpaper. I look down to see the couch cushions have transformed into actual sandpaper, scraping at my skin and my manly bits.

"Good 'un. Too bad I like it nude just as well," I say with a wink as I rip off my makeshift kilt without a care. Honestly, I can say that the one benefit of being a deer is getting used to having my junk hang out in all this cold. It doesn't even faze me when a gust of wind drifts in from a hole in the ceiling.

I hear a battle cry and am not at all surprised when Gus flashes by me, barreling into the ugly blue demon I've been annoying.

I watch them fight in midair. Gus swipes with his claws, and the unpleasant surprise demon flits in and out of time and space, just quick enough that Gus cannae touch him.

My eyes scan the room, lighting on trains and drums… and a bright pink microphone. I dive over to it, energized by an idea.

That's when I notice Cal and my Joy crouched behind some beginner electric guitar amps that will torture some poor parents' ears next year. Nostalgia hits me for a minute, because that was a key part of our plan for taking over Christmas. We were going to make sure every damn gift was so loud and obnoxious that parents all over the world would be annoyed by the very thought of Christmas day.

My eyes meet Cal's, and I do a quick check in. "You okay?" I ask.

"Yes. We're good," he responds.

Joy huffs, "If by good you mean we had to run from four of those fuckers because Bryn fell asleep, then yeah."

"Did Dem steal their weapons?" I whisper, as I reach for a little girl's microphone set, the kind that encourages obnoxious impromptu karaoke concerts that leave parents trapped on the couch with fake smiles for hours. It's a brilliant invention. I stroke it longingly before I wield it like the weapon it is, holding it up and searching for that little on switch.

"Yeah, but they're using their powers," Joy whispers as she tucks some blonde strands behind her ears and peers towards the Christmas cane, which seems way too far away. "One of them hit us with despair so bad, I thought I'd die."

"It wasn't that bad," Cal lies, adjusting his glasses.

We both just give him a deadpan look.

"We have to focus on that cane," he says, changing the subject rather than admitting his lie.

But he's right.

"You go. I'll annoy the crap out of them," I reassure them.

But a loud crash and the tinkling of falling glass undermine my words. I glance over to see Dem and one of the other demons grappling in midair, a cloud of dark magic all around them.

They crash into the teddy bear stuffing machine, denting it, before they ricochet into the giant 3D printer that Santa uses to create most of the plastic crap kids want these days. There's a dull thud as that machine falls and breaks.

A tear fills my eye suddenly, for no real reason, and my grip on the mic tightens.

Fook. That must be the despair arsehole fighting Dem.

Well, if you've got to feel depressed…might as well use it.

"Go!" I whisper urgently to Cal and Joy.

Then I flick that microphone on and start to belt out Whitney Houston's version of "I Will Always Love You."

Because what is more fooking frustrating and obnoxious than hearing some tone-deaf twat sing that song?

Immediately, I'm gratified to see annoyed expressions on every face as demons and angels alike reach to cover their ears. I get a thrill that perks up my dick as I spread my accent a bit thicker, like peanut butter, changing love into loooove.

Cal and Joy bolt for the cane, running at top speed.

And then, just as I'd hoped, one of the exterior doors to the workshop swings open and Bryn pokes in a very disgruntled head. "Hey! Some of us are trying to sleep!"

"Bryn, blast them!" I yell, foregoing the lyrics for a second.

Bryn's not the sharpest tack, the brightest bulb, the cleanest knickers…but when you need him, he's there.

A wave of exhaustion fills the room, and I swear, Sleeping Beauty's story must be the result of a sloth demon's work, because I blink my eyes once before I find myself tipping forward, too utterly spent to even put my hands out to stop my fall.

Right before my mind drifts into sleep mid-fall, I hope fervently that Bryn has enough sense to tie these fookers up.

Otherwise, I don't think we're going to have a very holly jolly good time.

14

JOY

THE DEMONS around me begin to drop like dominos, even Cal, who topples forward with his lips slightly parted. His eyes flutter before he seems to realize what he's doing.

"I'm sleepy," he murmurs, but he attempts to scramble to his feet again anyway.

Somehow, I seem to be the only person *not* affected by Bryn's sleepy power. I don't know if it's because I'm half-angel and half-human, or if it's because I'm his Center. Either way, I need to move. Fast. Before his spell wears off and I become target numero uno.

The cane almost seems to taunt me where it rests surrounded by plastic dolls with bleached-blonde hair and perfectly proportioned bodies. I can practically feel the power the cane exudes—power capable of ending this shit storm once and for all. Of freeing the cherubs and saving Christmas before the holiday crashes and burns in the fires of Hell.

I break into a run in the direction of the cane, my arm extending, my fingers mere inches away—

When something tackles me from the side. I hit the ground with an "oomf," pain reverberating through my body as the demon positions himself so he's straddling my waist. I recognize him immediately as the leader of the rival demon murder. Bangs, as I've named him in my head. His greasy blond hair flops over one eye as he holds a dagger up to my throat.

His eyes are hooded with fatigue, and I can tell that he's seconds from toppling over and falling into a deep, blissful slumber. However, the fucker seems determined to put me into an *eternal* slumber before that happens. Asshole.

"Such a pretty little thing," he purrs, and I can feel the sharp blade of his dagger caressing my cheek.

"Sorry, dude. I'm not into knife play," I hiss, struggling to come up with a solution to get myself out of this precarious position. I could wait until Bryn's magic consumes him completely, but I don't know how long that'll take. I don't know if he'll have enough time to slash my throat before he's consumed by the magic. And I happen to like my throat in one piece and, you know, not slashed, thank you very much.

"Stupid, insolent girl." He continues speaking in that soft, reprimanding voice, almost as if he's attempting to seduce me with his creepy words. Like, *hey, I have candy in my rustic van with the muffler falling off. Why don't you come inside and grab some?* I swear, the second I get free of this heavy asshole, I'm going to make him suffer. "Such a shame. Such a shame." He shakes his head sadly, even as his mouth opens in a wide yawn, one that reveals yellowing teeth embedded with black and brown gunk. Aren't demons supposed to be…attractive? Or something? I'm pretty sure I read somewhere that the devil designed her demons to be semi-attractive.

Obviously, I'm not dealing with the top brass here. Or maybe they're anomalies. Maybe that's how they defeated Dad. Their entire existence feels super off the books.

"You're going to die, Santa bitch." He throws his hand back, raising the dagger, and I prepare myself for death. Fuck, why does this have to happen to me? Why do I find males who are sexy and charming and adore me, and then fucking die? That's not fair. At all. Someone is going to get a stern talking to in the after-life, that's for damned sure.

For a brief moment, I close my eyes and allow the demons' faces to flicker behind my closed eyelids. These are men that I've barely gotten the chance to know but already mean the world to me. Cal's domineering presence and the way he takes charge of any and every situation. Gus's customary scowl that only seems to soften when he directs it at me. Yes, the fucker still scowls and glares at me, but there's a myriad of emotions behind that expression, emotions that send my heart into overdrive. Bryn's droopy smile and his warm cuddles. I always feel safe and protected around him, as if not even the fiercest snowstorm on Christmas morning can hurt me. And then there's Dem, with his sneaky ways. His pretty boy smile that makes me feel as if I'm the only person in the world worth stealing from. And finally, Nico. He embodies good-natured naughtiness. And some might call them evil, but to me...they bring smiles and laughter. And isn't that the point of Christmas? Happiness? I didn't even realize how much of that I was missing until Nico stomped into my life with his makeshift kilt and tangled red hair and lilting Scottish accent, fucking shit up and frustrating everyone in his presence.

My demons.

My mates.

And I'm going to die before this bond between all of us can truly develop into something more, something amazing and incredible and life-altering.

There's a whoosh of air, and a single tear trails down my cheek.

I'm sorry, Dad. I tried.

But the pain I expect never comes.

I hear a roar and snap my eyelids open.

Bangs is now lying on the floor beside me, knife knocked away, while a sleepy and disheveled Cal sits on his chest and throws punch after punch into his face. The punches get slower as my mate gets sleepier. But so do Bangs's reactions. The entire fight starts to look and sound like a slow-motion movie.

"No one." Punch. "Hurts my." Punch. Punch. Punch. "Mate."

"Fuck." Long ass yawn from Bangs. "You."

"Cal..." I breathe, sitting upright and placing a hand to my throat. I half expect my palm to come away red with blood because you don't always feel sharp knives. Luckily, my hand comes away dry.

"Go! I don't have him!" Cal punches the demon again. Both of their motions suddenly speed up, as if some of Bryn's sloth magic is wearing off. Despite the direness of the situation, I can't help but snort at Cal's contradictions. It'll be a different experience dating a demon who lies all the damn time, but I wouldn't have it any other way. Not when he also saves my ass.

I stumble to my feet, my pulse quickening when I see the rest of the demons getting up around the workshop. Apparently, Bryn's power has worn off everywhere, though the sloth demon himself is still fast asleep on a pile of brightly colored bean bags near the door.

I run toward the big container of dolls and yank the cane out of it, making several electronic babies start to cry when they tumble around. I grip the Christmas cane hard, reveling in the power just beneath my fingertips when I touch it, and stagger towards where the cherubs are beginning to wake up, still pinned to the ceiling like albino moths.

"Where's my father?" I demand when I'm close enough for them to hear me. When no one immediately answers, I reach for the nearest one pinned only ten feet off the wall—a girl I recognize as Jewels—and pat her shoulder with the hand not holding the cane. "Santa," I repeat curtly. "Where is he?"

She lifts a trembling hand and points towards a doorway that leads to his office. I waste no time racing in that direction.

If I can give Santa the cane, he can stop all of this. He can destroy the demons and save Christmas. He can save us all.

I shove open the door to his office, which is normally a gorgeous room with wood paneled walls and hunter green carpeting and a little fireplace behind his desk hung with stockings all year round. Only now, the walls are splashed with dried blood, the green carpeting is stained with a substance I really don't want to know the origins of, and the stockings are shredded.

"Oh, Dad!" I cry as soon as I catch sight of my father. He's hogtied in the corner of the room, his face covered in dark bruises and blood dripping from a wound on his head. His clothes are ripped, and some of his hair is even stained pink. Obviously, Bryn's spell reached him, even in a separate room, for his chest rises and falls steadily as he sleeps. The magic should have worn off, but maybe his injuries have kept him under. "Dad!" I shake his shoulder desperately, but he continues to sleep away, utterly oblivious to the mayhem just a room away. "Dad!" No response.

Fuck. Fuck. Fuck!

Maybe I can get Bryn here to wake him…

But we don't have time.

I can hear the growls and cries of pain as my demons fight once more, and I don't know how much longer they'll last.

Fear rakes across my back, and I turn away from Dad, holding the cane tighter. I hear a howl of pain from Cal that punts my heart right out of the office. A surge of adrenaline washes away my trepidation. I refuse to lose any of the men I've come to care about. I may be wary of them, I may be upset and confused about this whole reindeer thing, but they're still *mine*. My demons. My mates. My fucking future boyfriends.

Yes, I'm claiming them. I'm allowed to. I think after the shit day I've had, I can call these sexy as sin men mine. I'm not one for labels, but I'm firmly slapping one on all five of them. Right on their foreheads so the entire world can know who they belong to—me.

And if those demon assholes think they can hurt my guys, then they can go right on back to Hell. I'm happy to send them there.

"I love you, Dad," I whisper before I start to march back down the hall, swinging the Christmas cane in front of me like it's a bo staff. For Dad, I'll be brave. For my demons. For the cherubs. For everyone awaiting their presents Christmas morning. Because Christmas is all about hope and joy. And these fuckers want to deprive two separate realms of that. Not on my watch.

The toy shop…

It's a war zone. Gus and Ugly are in the middle of a fight in the air, howling like wild animals as they shoot dark jets of magic at one another. A slime machine has burst, its green guts oozing across the floor. There's a black spot where the harmonicas used to be made, and the scent of singed metal sizzles in my nostrils.

Blue battles Bryn and Nico on the ground. They're hurling plastic cars at each other. The miniature vehicles tumble through the air, careening off each other's bodies. A Jeep grazes Bryn's wing, and he lets out a roar of fury that startles even me. I don't think I've ever seen the sloth demon angry. Even as a reindeer, he was the most chill. Not now. He raises his hands and blasts Blue with some kind of sand magic. It hits the evil demon in the chest and sends him sliding backwards across the floor.

Cal is still throwing punches into Bangs's face, but they are at least ten feet from where they started, and there's blood dripping from a slash on Cal's shoulder, so Bangs has clearly gotten in several smacks of his own. Two of the rival demons are tied up in the far corner, knocked flat on their backs, snarling and hissing, while Dem unties their shoes and tosses them to the side. I don't know why the thievery demon is going for their shoes and not the swords on their backs, but I don't dare question his madness.

A burst of horrific grief rolls through the workshop, and I watch my guys sag as defeat drips like poison into their eyes.

Fuck.

No.

In a flash, the tide has turned. My guys curl into balls, go fetal. I hear Bangs chuckle evilly as he throws Cal off, as if he's been toying with him all along.

My own head is full of dark things. My mom, Ali's death, and her empty face. Dad's sad eyes for years after the funeral. I have to fight those thoughts off like they are demons themselves.

My hand grows slick on the Christmas cane. It trembles. I wet my lips with my tongue and slowly lift the cane.

You can do this, Joy. To save Christmas. To save Santa. To save your mates.

I hold the cane outwards and focus my energy into the swirling orb of green and red Christmas lights.

I instruct the magic not to hurt my mates or the cherubs. I tell it to target only the demons who wish to do us harm. I can feel the power coursing through my veins, setting my blood aflame, and I squeeze my eyelids shut as it rushes through me like a geyser being blown wide open. All at once, the magic shoots out of the glass, and five individual streams hit each of the bad demons, wrapping around their bodies like Christmas tinsel.

The force of the power sends me staggering back a step, but I don't allow my grip on the cane to loosen. I direct the flood of power at the demons, the magic cocooning them like wrapping paper...

"Holy fook." Nico. I'd recognize his accent anywhere.

I peel my eyelids open to see all of my demons back on the ground, staring at me in wide-eyed wonder. Besides a few bruises and scratches, they seem relatively unharmed. I can't help but breathe a sigh of relief. I don't know what I would've done if they'd been seriously injured, or worse.

And then I turn towards where Bangs and his crew once were, scattered throughout the workshop...

Only to see five Barbie dolls in their place.

Holy fuck is right.

I turned the demons into fucking Barbies.

15

JOY

"JOY TO THE WORLD!" the cherubs sing as my demons untie them. The poor things look utterly wretched after being trapped on the ceiling of the workshop for so long. They're a little loopy, so they don't even care that their carol makes no sense for this scenario.

At first, Santa's little helpers panic when I ask Cal and the guys to untie and fly them down to the floor, because their singed little wings just can't handle it.

"No! Don't do it, Joy! I'm sorry for all those times we called you a free willy whale!" Mittens nearly sobs. "Don't hand us over to more of them!"

A free willy whale? What the hell? That's an angel's derogatory name for someone who goes about doing whatever they want, regardless of the consequences. Other than a few dates here and there and some premarital orgasms, I've never done anything too bad!

But then, to angels who have a strict "hand only, unless you've sworn your soul to someone" policy, maybe a few dates are all it takes.

I try to stifle my irritation, because the cherubs are clearly traumatized. Like Dad always says, "People get weak. Sometimes, kids end up on the naughty list because they have poor impulse control. I always make exceptions for the ones who've had a really bad time. Because that's how you bring them back around to the good list."

So, with a deep breath, I smile gently at Mittens, a pudgy cherub with a little curl of nose hair that really needs a trim. "These demons are with me. They're not going to hurt you. They're going to rescue you."

Mittens shakes his head frantically, struggling to get out of Cal's arms and hover, despite the fact that his wings are far too injured to keep him afloat.

"MIttens, don't!" I scold, tossing out a hand as if I can catch him. But I'm still holding the Christmas cane. I absolutely cannot drop and break this cane because clearly our realm needs it! But I can't let him get hurt either, so I'm caught in a bit of a pickle.

Luckily, Nico and Dem fly over to help Cal.

"Shh, you'll be fine," Cal tells Mittens. For once, he's not lying. The sight of two more demons seems to startle Mittens for a moment, and my demon uses that distraction to carefully fly down, not even balking when the frantic angel wriggles and bucks like a wild little puppy in his arms. Cal simply proves the little guy wrong by bringing him down to safety.

After the others watch Mittens, they come much more easily.

Each of the demons treats the cherubs as if they're made of glass. They gently lower the little angels, navigating around all the smashed and cluttered tables, all the battle debris and broken toys, to set them in cleared spots on the ground not full of rubbish. Seeing the demons be so gentle makes my heart melt like caramel.

All appears to be going well, until the cherub in Nico's arms shrieks.

The others gasp and turn towards her, expecting the worst, like her being turned into angel stew or something else just as horrific, only to hear her erupt into giggles. She smacks Nico's finger away. "Do not be tickling my belly, you gingerbread head!" she yelps.

"Sorry, little lassie. My finger slipped." Nico's mischievous way of breaking the tension almost makes me laugh, but I don't know that the cherubs would appreciate it.

"All right, now we see if this thing will listen again." I hold up the cane skeptically, despite the fact that it just did exactly what I needed and pulled off an epic Christmas miracle. I'm still not quite sure that I've got the same amount of holiday in my heart that Dad does, so I don't know if the cane will work for me on a regular basis.

But I hold it up and try. To my astonishment and relief, a white light shoots out of it and envelopes the cherubs as an ethereal choir song fills the air.

I only have time to exchange a confused look with Cal, who shoves up his glasses and shrugs, before it's all over. The light dissipates, and the cherubs are left looking whole and hale. The cane's magic has healed them.

I clear my throat and get their attention, which feels weird. I've grown up around them, but I've never been in charge of anything more than snacks. A baker I may be, a leader I ain't. I'm pretty sure Shakespeare said that. "Um, so, I need you guys to split up and tell everyone that the threat is gone. Then we need to have a meeting to figure out what we're going to do about Christmas."

The cherubs all glance down the hall, and Mittens asks, "What about your dad?"

"He's next on my list, but he'll probably need a minute to deal with all of this." I wave a hand at the battle-strewn workshop, where all his centuries of hard work have been blown to bits.

Mittens's eyes fill with tears, a look of exhaustion passing over his pudgy cherub features, before he nods. "All right." He and the others fly out slowly, using one of the roll-up doors instead of the hole in the ceiling. It's probably just as emotionally taxing for them to see all their work in this state of shambles as it will be for Dad.

Guilt seeps into me then, as dark and disgusting as unflavored coffee, leaving a bitter taste on my tongue.

Did we try to save Christmas, only to ruin it?

My hand tightens on the cane as I walk back out of the main workshop, towards Dad's office. The hall doors are hanging from their hinges, and I gingerly sidestep them. I end up stepping on a whoopee cushion that got thrown in the battle, and a squeaky fart noise fills the air. I don't laugh, and not just because whoopee cush-ions are lame. I'm very worried at this moment that all of my work is going to result in something that's as pathetic as a whoopee cushion prank.

Is Dad going to be disappointed in me?

Did he expect me to do better than this? He's never had a problem vanquishing demons before. I mean, the guys around me are living proof of that. They've spent years as reindeer.

I get to the doorway of Dad's office and pause just outside, staring in at my disheveled, abused, still-sleeping father.

"Joy." Dem's voice pulls me out of my head. "Don't overthink it. Just heal him."

"Yeah, it's all going to be just fine," Cal reassures me.

I have to believe that. Whether it's true or not, it's what I need to believe right now. I lift the cane and hold it out towards Dad. As if it can sense Santa, a rush of magic immediately leaks from the ball at the top, this time, a sparkling gold whirlwind that surrounds my father, hiding him from sight momentarily before ceasing and revealing good ole Saint Nick, looking as rosy and bright as I've ever seen him.

He pushes up off the floor.

I rush forward and envelop him in a hug. "Dad," I whisper into his newly restored red coat. "I was so scared. I missed you."

Dad pulls back and looks at me, his eyes scanning the office. "Joy!"

I try to speak, but he pulls away and bolts down the hall before I can get out another word. I follow more slowly, only to find him standing just inside the doors of the workshop, a look of sadness marring his features. His forehead wrinkles as he surveys the destruction before his eyes settle back onto me.

"I'm sorry, Dad. We tried so hard, but they fought back and I'd dropped the cane in a snowbank—" I struggle to explain, the words tripping my tongue up as I try to figure out what I can say to erase that look of disappointment from his face.

His eyes fly to the cane in my hand, as if he's noticing it for the first time. "But...wasn't it broken? Didn't the Christmas cane break?"

"I built a new one," I tell him.

Dad's eyes get as round as the sugar cookies he always prefers me to make. "You built a new one?"

I nod. "I went to the divine realm and asked around. Got the ingredients and just—"

"Have I been out for a year?" Dad puts a hand to his head.

"No, goofy, just like two days," I tell him.

"Two days! You built a Christmas cane in two days!" Dad's jaw just about hits the floor.

I'm a little surprised he's so focused on the cane when I really thought that the destruction around us—or the demons standing behind me—would be a bigger deal.

"The battle in the workshop got a little out of hand, but we—"

"Where are the cherubs?" Dad asks.

"I sent the ones who were tied up to go tell the village everything is okay."

"You mean they weren't helping you?" Dad scrubs a hand over his face. "You did this alone?"

"What? No!" I spin around, only to see the demons aren't lined up behind me. "Guys?" I call out. "Guys?"

The demons step out from behind the rubble. Cal, of course, is the first to speak. "We thought we'd give you a minute of privacy."

Behind me, Dad launches to his feet and reaches for the cane. "Watch out, Joy! There are more—"

"Dad," I take a step back from him, worried that if he gets the cane, he might turn my allies, my mates, into Barbies.

He quickly moves to stand between me and the demons, his huge white wings ripping through his red coat.

I sigh as I start introductions, which look like they're going to go about as well as the time I introduced Dad to a narwhal shifter who liked The Clash. "You remember Comet, Cupid, Dasher, Donner, and Blitzen, right?" I ask casually. "Apparently, they're demons you turned into reindeer several years back."

"How'd they become human?" Dad demands.

I'm not really sure what happened there to be honest. So I skip over that question and move on to the important part. "They helped me turn those other dipshits into dolls."

"Language," Dad chastises automatically, but his eyes don't stray from them to me. Instead, he's giving them his meanest, most badass glare. "Joy, honey, did they try to get you to make a deal with them? What did they ask you for? You didn't make a deal, did you?" His fearful questions spill out one after another.

"No, they didn't ask for anything."

"Honey, don't lie! I'll help you get out of it, whatever deal you made." Dad turns to me with worry etched all over his face. He bites his lip, looking me up and down as if he can discern the deal just by staring at me.

"Dad, you don't understand…" I hesitate, because dropping this on Dad after everything doesn't feel right, but I don't have much choice. "I'm their Center."

If his jaw had been made of glass, it would have shattered. If he was a cartoon character, he would have fallen off a roof and turned into an illustrated white cloud and a *poof* sound effect. But since he's an angel,

Dad's eyes simply widen and his expression tightens into the most violent disapproval in all the realms. "Oh really? Is that what they told you?"

Cal steps forward. "It's true, sir," he says as he shoves his glasses up his nose.

"Demons don't let their Centers live, you liar!" Dad yells.

I've never heard him yell before. Not in my entire life. It's so loud that his words echo throughout the room, and I take a small step back, completely intimidated.

"We dinnae know she was our Center when we came, that's true. But now that we've lived with her for years, we've fallen in love with your daughter," Nico proclaims.

I know Bryn has said that they loved me, but I thought it was a spur of the moment kind of deal. Like, "hey, we might all die, but we should probably get these formalities out of the way."

But to hear Nico confess to my dad his undying love and devotion? That's a lot for my half-human heart to handle.

I'm not sure who is more surprised or terrified by that statement—me or Santa.

"Oh no you don't!" Dad growls. He yanks the Christmas cane out of my hands and points it at them.

"Back to reindeer. Or maybe candy cane poles this time, so you can't sniff around my daughter!"

"Dad!" I leap in front of the cane to block whatever magic he's about to send rushing at them. But no magic comes. The cane remains normal. The green and red swirling sparkles inside the bulb on top do nothing more than look like a festive snow globe.

Dad stares at the cane. "It's broken."

I shake my head. "No. I just used it to heal you."

"It can't be working. They're still fucking demons."

"Maybe it doesn't work on them because they just saved Christmas?" I suggest with a shrug.

"Gah!" Dad looks ready to pull out his own hair. His eyes fly towards my mates, and I'd be lying if I said he looked sane. He actually looks so red, he rivals a holly berry right now. "They probably knew that an angel's tears would turn them back into demons. They used you, Joy!" To the demons, he screams, "Leave! Leave this realm and never return or so help me—"

I interrupt what was probably going to be an epic threat, because as much as I love my Dad and want to keep this realm safe and whole, I do not want to continue using the Jollies app to find mediocre dates who make Victorian hair wreaths. Fuck that. If these demons are my mates, then this is my shot at happiness. And I'm not giving that up. "Dad. No. That's not happening."

Every eye in the room turns to stare at me.

"What?" Dad's brows crinkle like I just told him I signed up for the naughty list…which, maybe, possibly, I have.

But if this is what being naughty feels like, I don't think I'll ever want to be good.

"Sorry, Dad. But I'm half-human, so I'm pulling out the whole free will card here. The demons get to stay. We need to see if we click."

And for the first time in centuries, someone defies Santa Claus.

16

JOY

IT'S BEEN a long three weeks. A grumpy three weeks too, if you ask Santa. He's been eyeing my demons the entire time, suspicious of their every move, even though they've lived in a separate cabin from me and made every effort to help us repair and rebuild.

The workshop? Magic could only salvage a bit of it. Most of the machines are going to have to be rebuilt using good, old-fashioned hard work, because that's how God likes to set up all the realms. Whether they have magic or not, the beings on each planet have to work hard. Something about idle hands being the devil's plaything...

Dem came up with a solution for Christmas though. Everybody gets an iPad! He says it's literally one of the most coveted and stolen items on Earth. And guess what? That little mathematical branch of our new Christmas cane happens to do a great job of multiplying things. So, while we can't build entirely new workshops from scratch, we can replicate iPads until we have enough to fit the sleigh.

The five Barbies that I transformed? Well, they've got a special spot in Santa's Workshop. We've built them a shelf of their own right at the front near the door. It serves as a reminder of what we're doing and why it's so important. It also serves as a bit of amusement.

Every day, a new cherub's name is drawn and put on the board. That special angel gets to play with them for the day. The Barbies have had lots of tea parties, some very stellar weddings, and a few of them are even rumored by the cherubs to have Elf on the Shelf boyfriends.

Yes, angels have to be nice. To living creatures. Inanimate objects that might contain the souls of demons? Not so much.

They've really become a popular feature. Every cherub tries to outdo the last, and most of them wander by the Barbie shelf to see what's new each day. Yesterday, two of them were wearing white wings made out of toilet paper. Lots of photos were snapped.

I think that's a pretty fitting end for some assholes who wanted to take charge of Christmas. But while those demons are an open and shut case, my own demons are a bit more complex.

The guys have been trying. Key word, trying.

The first Monday after the incident, Bryn asked if he could eat lunch with me. I said yes despite Dad's giant frown. I met up with the cutie in my kitchen at the workshop, because I didn't really have time for much else. He was adorably flustered when he came in the door, and my heart had given a little leap when I saw how he'd tried to tame his normally sleep-rumpled hair. We'd sat at the counter with grilled cheese and milk, and he'd spent about twenty seconds complimenting my eyes before he fell asleep. I'd had to slide his glass of milk away so he wouldn't spill it.

Tuesday, Dem met me at the door of the kitchen, bright poinsettia wreath in his hand. "I got this for you." He'd grinned and helped me hang it on my door. Of course, an hour later, an angry cherub had flown in, demanding to know why I'd stolen the wreath she'd made.

Gus was too grumpy to hang around the cherubs and their caroling all day, so he'd taken to helping out around the stables, claiming that the cherubs there didn't pay proper attention to the animals and working out all his anger on mucking the stalls. I'd talked to him nearly every day, but he was silent and brooding for the most part. Once, he said, "You make my veins burn like I'm inside the sun." I still don't know if that's a compliment or if that's a wrath demon thing. I'm hoping compliment, because he did try to kiss me right after…but Dad.

He's always around! He's not giving me a fair shot at getting to know my soulmates. He doesn't trust them. And while I appreciate his fear and paranoia on my behalf, I also don't.

One demon I've seen every single day is Cal. He's been working with me to try to arrange for new transportation since the reindeer numbers are down now. I'd tried to get some heavenly llamas, but the angels who have them are really attached. He ended up calling in a favor with Lucillania herself and borrowing some hellhounds to help pull the sleigh, which makes Dad incredibly nervous. There's just no way these sweet guys can win with him it seems.

The one who's taken to the Christmas realm like a fish takes to water is Nico. He's come up with all kinds of ideas for gag gifts that kids would love, so he's been working with our gag department.

But our greatest obstacle by far has been my father. Kris Kringle doesn't like seeing his only daughter linked with demons. I could care less about the stares from the cherubs. But every time the demons mess up, Dad's there to point it out.

Like the day that Dem thought of a grand romantic gesture...

I awake to a clatter. I've hardly rolled out of bed before I hear someone pounding at my door. I slip on a fur cloak and some thick boots with a sigh and climb down from my loft to see what's the matter.

It's *way* too early for this shit. I haven't even had my morning hot chocolate yet, and we all know that hot chocolate is life.

"You have to see this!" Dem yanks me into the air as soon as I open the door, his smile blinding. I squint blearily into the blinding morning light. Though it's not as blinding as it usual is. Odd. It normally reflects off the snow...

I glance at the ground and realize there is no snow in front of my door. Only ugly, frozen dirt. My eyes trace the ground along the path that leads to my door. There's not a bit of snow in sight.

And considering I live in a place that has winter weather year-round, this is quite concerning.

"What happened?" I ask, as he slams my cabin door shut and then uses his wings to propel us through the air above the mud-packed path.

"I have a surprise!" Dem exclaims.

"A surprise?" I ask through a yawn. "Did you see the snow melted?" I eye the trees curiously, because they're still frosted with bits of snow like green sugar cookies. If the snow melted, then why...

At the end of the path leading to my cabin, the reason why there's no snow smacks me in the face. Almost literally.

There's a twenty foot tall snow sculpture at the end of the path. If the Abominable Snowman and Frosty had a baby, this would be it. It's a horrid, misshapen mass, and while I can see a protrusion that looks like a nose near the top, it does not look human at all. The only reason I can guess it's supposed to be human is the tablecloth that's been used as a scarf. There are a couple of boulders that I think are supposed to be eyes, but one's a bit droopy. The buttons look like more Christmas wreaths he probably "borrowed." It's truly the saddest snowman I've ever seen.

"I stole all the snow nearby and stayed up all night making it for you," Dem says softly as we land, still keeping his arms around me. "I know that when you were a little girl, you loved making snowmen. I heard the cherubs talking about it."

I turn in his arms to see his expression. My thief demon's eyes are soft, and his expression is vulnerable.

His lashes brush his cheeks as he looks down shyly underneath my scrutiny. His snow sculpture is atrocious...but the fact that he went to all this trouble for me...

My heart warms and sweetens like tea drizzled with honey. I lean forward to press a gentle kiss to his lips.

"You made me a snowman?" My voice hitches at the sudden surge of emotion that cascades through me.

"Well, since you're not allowed to play with my real balls yet..." He smiles softly, though a red flush has descended on his cheeks. "I decided to play with these snow ones for you."

"Weirdo." I curl my arms around his waist, until my breasts brush the fabric of his white shirt. The air around us thickens with anticipation and something else. Something deeper.

"Only for you," he breathes, his eyes flickering to my lips and turning molten with wanton need.

"Joy!" Dad's voice interrupts our sweet moment. "I need to go over some flight patterns with you."

I glance around Dem's dark wings, looking like obsidian stones in the sun, and towards the end of the driveway. Dad's standing on the road, clutching his cane. If he wasn't an angel, I think those eyes of his would spit fire.

Dem sighs and slowly untangles himself from my arms. Apparently, even my mischievous demon has a problem showing me physical affection in front of my father. But he leans in to whisper, "Do you like it?"

"I love it," I reply, giving him a long, soulful look. And I'm not talking about the snowman.

Dad's foot taps with increasing speed as he waits for me to leave Dem and join him.

Of course, Dad supplies a critique of the snowman as soon as we get into his office. I hold up a hand. "I don't want to hear it. He's trying. They all are."

Dad's nostrils flare, but he doesn't argue. Maybe he decides it will just make me dig my heels in, which it will. I sigh and work with him on flight paths until my eyes are crossing from staring at numbers for so long.

"I need a break," I tell him. "I'm going to make a batch of cookies. We can look at these again later." Dad nods and just pulls the sheaf of parchment closer to himself. I wish he'd ask Nico or one of my guys for help. Ha! Fat chance of that.

I reach the kitchen and sigh as I tie on my apron. I wish Dad would give my demons more of a chance.

"Oh, I ken frustration when I hear it, lass. I love that emotion rolling off of you. You're growly and hot,"

Nico drawls. "But I suppose it's not a feeling you really want, now is it?"

My Scottish demon has wandered in from outside, stomping the snow off his boots. He looks a bit wild today, his red hair disheveled, his black wings dusted with snow. He's wearing a red kilt and a black sweater, but quickly yanks the sweater off over his head to my delight, revealing only a thin, nearly transparent white T-shirt beneath. The material clings to his pecs in delicious and tantalizing ways.

He pulls a stool up to the countertop and rests his upper body on his elbows, leaning over the granite surface. "What's wrong lass?"

I bite my lip and fidget with a set of measuring spoons on a ring, pulling my attention away from my handsome mate and focusing on the problems at hand. "It's Dad. I don't know how to get through to him."

Nico nods. "Yeah. He's got a thrawn sense of self."

"What?" Sometimes, his Scottish words throw me for a loop.

Nico gives me an easy grin. "He's a bit of an obstinate bastard."

I laugh harshly. "That's true." As soon as my laughter ends, my throat tightens. I wish it wasn't. I wish that

Dad would accept that these men are amazing and that they're my soulmates.

Suddenly, Nico is right next to me. "Ah, dinnae cry. I canna handle it." His big hands cup my shoulders and gently rub them before he pulls back. "I have an idea. Wait there!" He flies out my door a second later, not even bothering to put his sweater back on.

Just a moment later he's back, shaking snow off himself and slamming the door shut. A"It's fooking cold outside!"

"Well, it is the Christmas realm," I reply drily.

"Smart alec." Nico stomps over to me, and I can fully appreciate up close that the snow has made his white T-shirt damp.

Yes, those frigid nipples of his are clearly visible, and suddenly, my personal oven is on pre-heat.

"Do ya have a lighter?" Nico holds up a twig he must have just snapped off of a tree. A juniper berry still clings to it.

"Of course." I shuffle through my drawers, not bothering to ask what he's doing, just hoping to prolong the moment with a hot demon competing in my own personal wet T-shirt fantasy. I take a little longer than necessary to find the lighter, possibly because my eyes hardly hit the drawer.

When I go to hand the lighter over, instead of taking it, Nico's hand wraps around my own, squeezing the lighter into my palm. "Let's do it together," he breathes.

"What are we doing?" I ask as my entire body lights up like a Christmas tree at his touch.

"In Scotland, there's a Christmas tradition. You burn a rowan twig to get rid of any bad feelings someone might have towards yer."

He moves his thumb over the wheel, and the lighter sparks with a tiny little flame. Nico holds up the twig above the counter and slowly brings the two together. Both of our eyes watch as the flame meets the Christmas twig, and the scent of juniper fills the kitchen. I find myself wishing with all my heart that Dad can see the good in these demons. Because to me, it's there, as bright and clear as the North Star.

When the twig has shriveled to nothing, Nico releases my hand and turns towards me. His expression makes my breath hitch and a soft, "Thank you for sharing that with me," emerges.

His smile grows tender. "Ah, lass, I wanna share everything with you." He leans down, his giant form bending, his lips lowering to mine.

"What do we have here?" a jolly voice interrupts.

For once, it's Cal, not Dad, ruining the moment. I turn to him and put both hands on my hips, even as I still clutch the lighter. "That was rude."

"I'm so sorry," Cal responds, hand flying to his chest.

"Nae, you're not." Nico sighs and straightens. "I'd better get back to it, before the old man accuses me of being a skiver and not pulling me weight." He grabs his sweater but carries it in his hands, not putting it back on as he walks to the door, perhaps because he knows my eyes follow him like a heat-seeking missile zeroing in on its target.

He gives me a wink and a nod, and then, he's gone quick as a flash.

I turn back to Cal and point the lighter accusingly at him. "Don't go ruining my romantic moments with the others on purpose."

He holds up his hands innocently. "I wasn't." But when he sees my eyes narrow at his obvious little white lie, he changes course. "Okay, I was. I was jealous. I want you to stare up at me that way." He shoves his glasses up his nose and gives an adorable pout.

"I do, you goof. All the time. Plus, you get more time during the day than the others right now. So be nice."

He pretends to pout as he comes closer. "Fine. Now, will you tell me what that was all about?"

"We burnt a twig in the hopes it will help Dad come around."

"Oh, your Dad already loves me, Joy. It'll all be just fine."

Unfortunately, both of us know that's a lie.

TONIGHT IS A BIG STEP FORWARD—DINNER WITH DAD.

I gulp nervously as I stare into the mirror. I've chosen a gold dress for the occasion. It's got a white fur collar and cuffs and is very conservative. Because even though I've been defying Dad's wishes and dating my demons, I'd really, really like his blessing.

They know it too, which is why they arrive half an hour early at my cabin. And every single one of them is wearing a suit in official Christmas colors. They even stand side by side in alternating red and green, a feat that I'm certain was planned.

My eyes flit over each of their faces in the moonlight. All of them but Gus wear a nervous grin. Gus has his customary scowl in place, but his tattooed fingers are tapping at his pant leg, revealing his unease.

"Hi," I say shyly, even though I saw a lot of them just this morning at the workshop.

"You look gorgeous." Bryn gives a dreamy sigh.

"Thanks." I grin.

"Can we come in for a minute?" Cal asks, a smooth smile on his face as though he's not nervous at all and looking forward to being grilled by an angel. The expression is a lie, but a sweet one.

I pull my door open and watch them all stomp their boots to rid them of snow before they head towards my fireplace.

"Any tips for dealing with your father?" Dem asks pretty much as soon as I shut the door.

I've been thinking about this a lot, actually. How to get Dad to like them. So far, he's resisted, no matter the help they've given him and Christmas Village as a whole. He insists they're going to kill me or leave me, that they're lulling me into a false sense of security.

I'm pretty certain he's tried to turn them all into Barbies on multiple occasions, but the cane still won't stand for it. Thank goodness magic is apparently loyal to its makers.

"Well, Dad is kind of a workaholic, so honestly, I feel like all the hard work you've been putting in would have convinced him." I chew my lip, and a part of me wants to play with my hair, but I just spent an hour spraying and curling it to perfection, so I don't touch it.

We spend a couple of minutes brainstorming options that range from turning Dad into a candy cane light post—which I vehemently object—to continuing to slow-play our relationship, which has been ridiculously hard. It's only been three weeks, but I swear I have finger pain from the number of times I've jilled off after a sweet little date with one of them. Just this afternoon, Dem stole my spatula right as I was about to pull cookies off a cookie sheet, and I had to chase him around to get it back. Then, he'd stolen a kiss and my breath.

My fingers had gone to work as soon as I'd gotten home tonight, remembering the naughty look in his eyes.

"No getting a horny face right now," Gus grumbles.

Nico agrees. "He's about two seconds from kicking us out of this realm, lass. He's just waiting for us to make a mistake. I can feel it as sure as the sun."

I close my eyes and try to clear my head. "You're right. Sorry." I swallow hard. Ugh. They've been trying to be good. The refuse to do more than kiss me, which frustrates the fuck out of me because they're demons. They aren't meant to be good. And my own naughty side wants them to act on this attraction between us.

Cal steps forward, his eyes calm and his smile placid. "Don't worry about it, Joy. I've got a plan." I don't think he's lying. And that makes me very, very nervous. Because what kind of plan could a demon have when being good doesn't work?

A bad one.

WE'RE ALL SEATED AROUND A THICK MAHOGANY TABLE. White candles flicker in silver candelabras, and 1920s instrumental Christmas music plays through a phonograph because when he's not working, Dad prefers the scratch and texture of old records. He loves items that were made by hand, not machine. It's the craftsman in him.

In front of me, a bowl of lobster bisque sits uneaten, the smell a tempting spice, but my stomach is as chunky as half-mixed cookie dough.

Dad's frowning at Dem's explanation of his history. How he worked his way up the ranks of Hell by stealing the credit from other demons. Dad hears stealing and just shuts down. He doesn't recognize Dem's brilliance. He doesn't see how clever Dem was to not commit any of his apparent crimes, but just slide in at the last moment and claim them as his own. Dad's missing the point. The point is that Dem isn't nearly as bad as he thought.

"I brought you a gift," Bryn says, trying to jump in and dilute the tension.

Dad's eyes widen a bit, and I can tell he's caught off guard.

Yes! Hope buds in my stomach as my adorable sloth demon passes over a red box with a bow to Dad.

Dad can't help but smile. He does love gifts. He undoes the bow and lifts the lid, his smile freezing on his face. "What is this?" he asks, pulling out a sugar cube.

Oh no. I have a feeling I know where this is going. And I don't think it's going to be good.

"Sugar," Bryn replies with a wide, lazy smile, oblivious to the fact that everyone else in the room just tensed. "The first time I saw your daughter, she fed me a sugar cube, so I thought…"

"You thought to remind me of the fact that I should have turned you all into holiday doormats instead of reindeer? Then this whole debacle might never have—"

"Dad!" I interject, my cheeks flaming. I cannot believe he just said that in front of my mates! "If they hadn't been around to help me, we never would have been able to build a new Christmas cane! Bryn carried the water of innocence in his mouth!" I don't mention that he was carrying my innocence-soaked panties, because that's a detail no father ever needs to know.

Dad's cheeks get rosy with his own temper, and his wings twitch. We are about to have a full-fledged argument when Cal's voice slides across the table, as smooth as butter.

"Mr. Kringle, I know that we're not conventional mates for your daughter. We're not the typical sort of beings that live in your realm."

Dad's eyes flicker over to Cal and narrow. I grab my soup spoon and briefly contemplate trying to slit my wrists with it. Yes. With a spoon. That's how uncomfortable I am right now.

"So, we've discussed it. And if you require it, we'd be willing to ask Lucillania to release us from our positions as demons so that we can be with Joy."

Both Dad and I let out audible gasps. The moment of shock drags on as a trumpet plays a little bit of a jazz solo in the background, oblivious to the fact that my guys just offered to give up their magic, their purpose...for me.

"Really?" Dad's face gets contemplative.

I stand up and wield my spoon like a weapon, waving it at Dad. "No. Don't even! Just. No." I turn to my guys. "I really appreciate your offer, but I can't let you do that. I can't have you give up who you are. I can't make you change, just for me. That wouldn't be right. The offer, though, the fact that you'd be willing..." I trail off as I get a bit choked up. My eyes grow annoyingly misty as I try to make eye contact with each one of them and thank them with my gaze. "It's the best gift that anyone's ever given me. I love you all so much."

Behind me, Dad grumbles, tossing his napkin on the table beside his bowl as though he's suddenly lost his appetite. "You're clever, I'll give you that. Gah! Fine. You've got my blessing. But you can't touch my girl until you've sworn your souls to her. And that's not happening until after Christmas."

Cal looks my Dad straight in the eye. "Yes, sir. I promise."

17

JOY

Finally, Christmas Eve is here. Dad is gone. And he will be gone ALL. NIGHT. LONG. We just saw him off, and he was hardly through the veil before I turned to the demons and asked if they wanted to come back to my place.

They said yes, and now I don't know if I really love or really hate my temporary moment of bravery. Dad's edict has been torture. But…I'm also nervous. I swallow hard as we walk towards my cabin, and the moonlight glints off the snow so that it looks like sparkling mounds of sugar. "Baby It's Cold Outside" starts to play inside my head, along with all the innu-endo imbued in the lyrics of that song.

I should be shivering since the temperature has dropped, but I'm surrounded by my soulmates and they radiate a heat that seems to come right from the fires of Hell. Or maybe that's just me. Maybe I'm just flushed with excitement. The excitement of success and anticipation of what might come next.

I'm buzzing with nervous energy, drunk on giddiness, and pretty certain I'm about to stupidly giggle for no reason other than these demons are here…surrounding me. I've realized that I love them…a lot.

"That look on their faces was priceless!" Dem exclaims, and we all nod in agreement.

"I hope some little lass with a mean big brother gets those Barbies and uses them for combat games," Nico comments.

"I don't," Cal returns. "I hope they find a very sweet little girl…" We all turn to give him sarcastic looks because that lie is just the worst ever, but then he continues, "one who likes to dress them all up and give them extra makeup, who'll give them haircuts and make them have lots of tea parties and weddings."

"Ugh! Torture!" Bryn shudders.

"Exactly." Cal winks.

All of us start to laugh, except for Gus, but his lip quirks up a little, like maybe he wants to join. But do wrath demons laugh? Are they even physically able to do so?

We keep walking in companionable silence, and the battle starts to replay a bit in my mind, this time with the golden glaze that memory gives victory, the way that it paints everything a bit grander than it actually was.

These guys and I kicked some pretty righteous ass together. And that creates a bond, right? Well, maybe we already had that bond. I don't know. I've never been a Center before. But this happy little tingle that runs from my chest to…other places is amazing.

To be honest, I'm looking forward to reaching my cabin more than a kid looks forward to Christmas morning.

From underneath my lashes, I glance at the demons around me, the men who've been my companions for years and who now are suddenly my mates. That's so utterly strange. But at the same time, it's not. It explains why all of those dates I've been on have sucked in comparison to hanging out in the stable and brushing them.

Part of me is relieved I'm not destined to be a llama lady, like some of the angels in Heaven who decide not to join a flock and don't find their Centers. They end up with entire herds of llamas. One angel I know has twelve. Hell, I was one bad date away from getting a lifetime subscription to the local llama chew toy and gourmet food box.

A future without crappy dates…

That thought shines like a beacon from a lighthouse. Instead, I can get cuddles on the couch at my leisure. All the good morning kisses I've been saving up will finally get put to use. And…I hope…orgasms on demand.

Are they thinking what I'm thinking?

Because I'm thinking about getting a whole lotta presents under *my tree*.

Bryn is in front of me, his steps quicker than I've ever seen him. But is he hurrying to get to the warmth of the cabin for a nap…or for other reasons? I can't see his face and tell if his eyes are hooded or droopy.

Suddenly, I start to reevaluate all the long stares he gave me when he was stuck as a reindeer. I always thought he was staring off into space, half-asleep, but maybe I was wrong. I hope I was.

Part of me wants to dart in front of him just so I can see his expression. But I don't. I feel shy about that for some reason. I've never been shy around them before.

But come the fuck on? How many more clues do they need? Should I just put wrapping paper on my pussy with a huge green and red bow? Maybe a card that says, "Open"? Would they finally understand what I want then?

Beside me, Gus takes my hand in his. His huge, rough palm encases my fingers, and his thumb gently strokes my skin. Can he tell I'm nervous? It's a sweet gesture from a guy who looks ready to murder most people at any second, with his black wings, tattoos, the ring on his lip... I find myself glancing at that ring more than once.

He gazes down at me with this fierce intensity, but I'm not quite sure if it's lust or fury. It's hard to tell with him. I turn to see if the other demons are easier to read.

Cal and Nico are on my other side, chatting softly. Both of them have wide smiles on their faces, their black wings folded back, just like the cherubs or dragon shifters fold their own wings back casually. The only difference I can see between these two and angels are their wings and horns. Cal's horns are a dull brown and thin like twigs. They almost look like antennas on his head. With his glasses, his tiny horns give him a cute, nerdy, bumblebee look that I would never in a million years admit to him.

Nico's horns look like some kind of spiral seashell in shades of gray, which contrast his bright red hair. His chest hair is curly and red too, with a few freckles sprinkled over his skin. I've never been with a redhead before, and the sight of those freckles does odd things to me. I want to kiss each one. I want to trace them with my fingertips and my tongue.

I glance back so that I don't give into the urge and reach out to touch Nico, because if I do, I'm pretty sure I won't want to stop and I'm not interested in a make-out session in a snowbank. Tried it when I was a teen and nearly froze my nipples off. Never again.

Dem walks behind me, but I feel his presence like he's trailing a feather up my spine. He's one of those men that can only be described as beautiful, a pretty boy, with long lashes and such a smile…

I turn forward after he gives me a grin that makes my lady parts holler. I've never been so utterly aware of five men before. But they surround me and fill me with so much damn heat that I'm surprised the snow isn't turning into puddles under my feet.

I swallow hard, thinking of how much I owe them. I've said thank you at least a dozen times over the past few weeks, but even that doesn't feel like enough. Without these men, my home wouldn't exist anymore. And so, despite the fact that I probably sound like a broken record, I say it again. "Thank you for saving my home." My voice comes out breathy because I'm so full of emotions.

"Our home," Bryn corrects with a giant yawn. I glance over at him as he stretches his muscular arms skywards, and my heart gives a girlish sigh of contentment.

Our home.

Do they really feel that way? Are they…staying? Is this going to be more than just victory sex? I know I'm picturing lazy mornings and matching plaid pajama pants, but are they? And what is going to happen at my cabin, which is rapidly approaching? Are we going to… I don't even know. I've only ever been with one guy at a time before. I mean, I've read about other things, but…

"Wanna bake cookies?" Bryn turns to me with a grin and stifles a yawn behind his hand. "I'm really hungry."

That statement makes my anticipation morph from nervous mathematical impossibilities—five dicks plus one of me equals intimidating—to wondering how many cups of sugar I have left in my kitchen and if it will be enough to make them each a batch of their favorite cookies, which is absolutely the least I can do in order to thank them for everything they've done.

A thought occurs to me, and I jerk to a stop, forcing Gus, who still has my hand, to stop too. All of the guys turn to me in alarm.

"What's wrong?" Gus scans the horizon for threats.

"Do you guys actually *like* my cookies?" I ask. And this is a nerve-racking ask for me, because there was a bear shifter once who told me my cookies were shit after we'd been together for two months. Dad made sure he got coal in his stocking for the next three years after the sob-fest that occurred. Liking my cookies is kind of a deal breaker for me. My cookies are my self-expression. They're kind of my art. They're my love language.

The silence doesn't even stretch on, but the tiny bit of time they take to look shocked makes my gut start to churn.

Oh no. I can't have mates who don't like my—

"Hell yes!" Bryn exclaims.

"Your cookies are the bomb!" Dem snorts as if it's completely obvious.

Still, I turn and eye the others. "You really like them? Even the sugar cookies?""

"Especially the sugar cookies," Cal says as he shoves his glasses up his nose.

"That's a fookin' lie. His favorite is chocolate chip, but he canna help it, so dinnae be too mad," Nico reassures me. "But we like them all the same. You think we'd crowd your kitchen if we dinnae?"

"I mean, you were reindeer, so maybe things tasted different…" The most brilliant of all ideas comes to me.

"Ohhh, I know what we're going to do." A wide smile stretches across my face.

All the guys stop and stare at me for a second, like they're frozen.

I take a second to make eye contact with each one of them. "We're going to cook a bunch of different kinds of cookies, and then we're going to have a blind taste test. I want to see which ones are your favorites!"

"Mine are–"

I cut Gus off, even though it makes him glower at me. I squeeze his hand as I say, "Don't tell me! It'll ruin the fun!"

"But Nico just told you Cal's." Dem shakes his head with a wry smirk tilting up his lips.

"Then I'll search for his second favorite," I respond, already excited enough to clap my hands together. This will be perfect. It will give us the chance to chat and get to know each other and for me to figure out exactly what having a Center means to them.

Bryn opens the door to my cabin and holds it like a doorman, doing an adorable little arm sweep as he says, "Your castle, my lady," and tries not to yawn.

"Thank you, evil sir." I wink, and his grin makes his cheeks flush.

"So, you want some help?" Cal asks, once we're all in my living room. "I'm an excellent sous chef."

I can tell he's lying, but it's so damn sweet of him to offer. "Sure," I say, detangling my hand from Gus's. The wrath demon gives a discontented growl until I turn and glance up at him. "Gus, honey, you think you and Dem could start the fire?"

I swear, at the word "honey" his eyes dilate and his breathing stops.

"Yeah." His voice is gruff, and he quickly turns and walks over to the fireplace. It's the best part of my little cabin. Two stories of smooth river stone, it heats up the entire little place in a jiffy. I love the orange glow it gives the wood beams too. It makes it feel cozy.

I have to tell myself not to stare at Dem's ass when he bends to put a couple of logs in my fireplace. I then also have to tell my dirty mind not to think of logs in the fireplace as a naughty metaphor. Especially not several logs.

Oh, my libido is out of control. I just want to get to know these demons. We aren't *there* yet. A couple of random lunch dates don't count.

I head over to the kitchen in the corner. It's not as spacious or well-equipped as the one in the workshop, but it's fun and it'll get the job done.

I open a cabinet and start pulling out ingredients. Immediately, Nico's at my side.

"Here, lass, let me help." He brushes my hand with his as he takes my bag of sugar.

Why does that make my throat dry out? A simple brush of his hands? It must be a Scottish thing.

"What can I grab?" Bryn asks cheerfully, his eyes hooded.

"Butter," I rasp, very aware that Cal has just boxed me in from the other side, his pecs brushing my shoulder. When did he lose his shirt?

"Don't leave me out," he adds. "I want to have a hand in this."

Yes, my brain turns that dirty as well.

"Can you get the mixer?" I ask him, not moving, because who would move away from pecs that are as solid as granite? Especially those that are bare, because the demon is only wearing pants right now. His nipples could cut glass...or maybe even my tongue if I licked them.

Which I won't, I tell myself. Not until I find out their intentions. Of course, I also call myself a spoilsport.

"Oh, yeah, the mixer is in the bottom cabinet, right?" Cal asks.

I realize, like a complete idiot, that I'm standing in front of that cabinet. "Oh. Um, yeah. Let me just move—"

His hands on my shoulders make me freeze. "Don't move. I'll get it." He comes to stand in front of me, and then his hand touches my waist. "Spread your legs."

Oh God.

I spread them, and Cal slowly squats down, letting his hand trail over the front of my dress and then the top of my thigh. His touch burns me up, and my eyes can't leave him when his hand reaches between my legs and pulls open the cabinet door. The door shoves against my skirt, and he tsks.

"Nico, could you pull her skirt up a little please, so I can get in here?" Cal looks up, his expression a lie—it's the picture of innocence.

"Of course." Nico gives me a sultry grin as he turns to me. "If the lady doesn't mind."

I shake my head. Mind? No I don't mind. I don't even *have* a mind to mind anymore. It flew outside somewhere and buried itself in the snow. All I have left is a greedy pussy who is screaming for someone to touch her.

"Hands on the counter, lass," Nico says softly.

My hands grip the edge of the countertop like they've been superglued. They are absolutely not moving an inch.

"Oh, Joy likes to be a good girl," Bryn observes from the other side of the kitchen. His hooded look has turned sly.

My heart starts clanging like a tambourine as Nico's hands come to my hips and he slowly hikes up my skirt. The drag of the material against my skin is the worst sort of tease. It's a soft, delicate touch of fabric. But I want another kind of touch right now.

My eyes drift down to Cal's face. He's kneeling between my knees, his eyes firmly planted on my thighs, knowing what's about to come. My very bare pussy. Because ever since we've gotten back to Christmas Village, all of my panties have gone missing. I don't have a single pair left. It's almost like someone has stolen them all.

I have an inkling who might do such a thing, but I haven't called him out on it, maybe because a part of me thinks it's nice to be a little naughty.

When Nico finally pulls my skirt up high enough for Cal to see my pussy, he gasps.

"An actual Christmas tree?" he asks, staring at the tiny shape I've left with my pubic hair.

I blush. "Well, presents go under the tree, right?" My cheeks burn as I explain my logic. God, I'm dumb.

But not one of the guys smiles. Cal looks up at me, and his eyes are ringed in demonic red as he says, "We're going to give you so, so many presents."

And I'm pretty sure that's the truth, not a lie.

I tense in anticipation when his hand reaches between my legs, already imagining how soft his thumb will feel. But Cal doesn't touch me. To my utter disappointment, he actually does pull out the mixer.

Nico drops my skirt and steps back as Cal stands, Kitchen Aid mixer in hand.

"Dinnae look so disappointed there, missy," Nico whispers in my ear. "If you stay on our good list, you'll get lots of presents."

I bite back the urge to stick my tongue out at him. But damn.

"You all are mean," I accuse.

Dem strides into the room, back lit by the fire, which is crackling merrily. The most beautiful of them all, he whips his shirt off. "It's a little hot in here now, isn't it?" He grins at me. And then he drops his pants.

I gape. I've watched lots of porn. Hell, I've slept with dragon shifters, who are as buff as they come. But

Dem's level of gorgeous? I've never experienced anything like it before. I'm stunned. He's like one of those ornaments covered in glitter that's just completely hypnotizing.

"Well, what are you waiting for?" Dem winks. "I need a cookie, stat!"

I'm supposed to bake while he just hangs out? Literally?

"This is a horror movie come to life!" I mutter as I turn to grab a jar of cinnamon, blowing a breath out and telling myself that I do have some self-control.

"Are you calling my dick a monster?"

"He'd be the tiniest monster in all of existence," Cal quips.

"We all know that's not true," Dem retorts as he kicks off his shoes and pants, moving around the counter so I can see him in all of his glory up close as he cuffs Cal over the head.

Immediately, they start to grapple with each other.

"Hey!" I call out. "None of that in my kitchen! If you want to do it on a bearskin rug in front of my fireplace and pretend I'm watching some kinky adult channel... well then, go ahead."

That makes all five of them turn to me and grin madly. "Think we've got her riled up?" Bryn asks, pride evident in his tone. For once, he doesn't look on the verge of sleep.

"Oh, yeah." Dem grins.

I shake my head. "Whatever happened to the 'get to know you conversations' that are part of the first bit of dating?"

"We've known you for years, lass," Nico responds. "Know your favorite color is yellow, despite all this red and green getup you've got going in honor of your dad."

"I know that you sleep on your right side every night," Bryn adds, tucking his hair back before leaning his elbows onto the countertop and giving me a lazy grin.

"How do you know that?" I query.

"We've flown up and peeked into your window a time or two," he responds, not at all ashamed or embarrassed.

"I know you hate when the fucking cherubs don't finish their cookies," Gus tells me, finally joining the conversation as he leans against the wall, his tattooed body so dark, it's like a shadow. "It makes you want to punch them out."

I turn to him, aghast. "*You* never finish your cookies." He's the one who's made me the most insecure about my baking these past few weeks.

He grins. An actual, real-life grin from a wrath demon. "I know. I love it when you get pissed. It's hot."

Hellfire must rain down on my vag right then, because that level of devious combined with his rare smile sets me off. Damn.

"You are *naughty*," I tell him with a smile.

"Yes, I am." He slides his shirt off. "And you're more beautiful than all the stars combined."

The other guys all turn and stare at him for a second. He doesn't take his eyes off me, his irises turning a gorgeous, gleaming red.

Then Dem walks over and stands behind Gus. Dem peeks over Gus's shoulder and folded black wing at me as his arms slowly circle Gus's waist. I'm entranced as he slowly undoes Gus's belt, then sensually slides the other man's pants down. He deals with Gus's shoes, but I don't notice those. I'm too distracted by the tattoos that line Gus's abs all the way down to his cock. My eyes can't help but trace the patterns of the tribal designs inked into his skin, but they also keep going back to that thick dick, the tip of which is pierced.

Pierced.

There are naked demons in my kitchen. I bite my lip and remind myself that I want to know more about them. Not their cocks. Them.

"Okay, what are your hobbies?" I ask before cringing.

"I like Scrabble," Cal says.

"Nobody likes Scrabble," Dem replies, rolling his eyes and stepping out from behind Gus to face me. At least, I think he rolls his eyes. When I look over at him, I have trouble focusing on his face, despite how gorgeous it is, because his dick has started to get hard.

I suddenly feel all that heat the guys talked about. The weather outside might be frightful, but in my cabin, it suddenly feels like the tropics. Hot and wet.

"Well, for the past several years, eating hay and avoiding stepping in shit, those have mainly been our hobbies. Oh, and stalking you," Bryn adds. "And sleeping."

"Right. Duh. Sorry." I look around. "Anyone want wine while I bake?"

"I'm thirsty," Cal says.

I turn to grab a cup, but he stops my hand. "I'm thirsty, but not for wine." He comes over and grabs me by the waist. He spins me around and sets me on top of the counter so that my legs dangle. "I wonder, is there anything besides wine I could drink in this kitchen?" he asks, his eyes dancing with mirth.

I play innocent. "Water?"

Gus comes around and pushes my ribcage gently back until I'm lying on the countertop. "I don't know about drinking, but I do know that my favorite flavor of cookie is about to be served."

My chest heaves, my nipples tighten, and my thighs clench as I feel Nico and Dom slowly slide my skirt up.

Gus leans in even closer, his lip ring brushing my ear as he says, "And I don't think I'll stop eating this cookie until it's *all done.*"

18

JOY

CHRISTMAS IS A SEASON FOR GIVING, and boy, do my demons give a lot. They don't even give me a chance to get nervous because they all surround me up on the counter, five sets of eyes burning with a need that melts my core.

Gus nips at my neck before licking a red-hot stripe up the side that leaves my pulse pounding. He moves to the side of my countertop, freeing up the space between my legs, before lowering his lips again to my pulse. Bryn starts to do the same on my other side, though his technique is much more languid than Gus's. His tongue traces swirls along my neck, which contrast with the little teeth tracks Gus starts to make.

It feels dark and delicious, decadent as a black and white cookie. Between the sensations rolling through my body and my anticipation about what is going to come next, I feel like I'm teetering, walking along the edge of a cliff. It's an addictive sensation.

Someone yanks down the top of my dress, ripping it, but I don't care. I'm eager, excited, when two hands scoop my breasts out of the cups of my bra. A thumb starts to brush over my right nipple, and it tightens, shooting sparks right down my center.

"Fucking hell," I mumble.

"Damn straight," Dem responds. "You think anything from Heaven could feel this good?"

I chuckle, but only for a moment because something rubs along the inside of my calf, and I'm not sure what it is. It heats up all the nerves along my leg, making them crackle with excitement. I lean up a tiny bit so that I can look down, and I realize that Cal is playing with my breasts while Dem has knelt between my legs and is rubbing his horns on me. His horns are a purple shade so deep, they almost look black. His horns curve out to the side, and then up near the tips, so they look like a bull's horns. But instead of being hard, they're covered with the softest little baby-duck fuzz, so that it feels like a velvet covered dildo is sliding along my skin. And his horns are hot. So damn warm that I can feel the heat from them on my pussy.

If he's not careful, my Christmas tree is gonna catch on fire.

My eyes light on Nico, who's standing in front of an open cabinet and drizzling some olive oil onto his finger. The huge Scottish demon catches me watching him and sets down the bottle before he lewdly spreads the oil up and down his own finger.

I almost lift my hips towards him to beg him to put that finger on me, until he says, "You get to choose where this finger goes, lass, but choose wisely. Once it's there, it's not leaving until I decide it is."

That makes me gulp. I was going to have him touch my clit, but the others already have me so close…and I'll get so sensitive after. Should I ask him to put it in my ass instead? There are five of them. Indecision makes me silent.

Nico's eyes dance with wicked glee as he waits patiently. But there is nothing patient about my other mates. Cal's head dips and he sucks my nipple into his mouth, his tongue toying with me. When his teeth nip at me, a tiny zap of pleasure shoots towards my clit, but isn't enough to spark it into a full orgasm, I shout, "Clit!" without any ability to consider the consequence of my actions.

The second Nico's hot, oiled finger slides back my hood and touches my sensitive bundle of nerves, I nearly cry in bliss. Warm tingles start to overwhelm me, and when Gus leans over to capture my lips with his, I pour all of my moans into his mouth. His lip ring is cold against my chin as his lips move over mine. A hand, I assume it's his, fists my hair and tugs it hard. That sharp pull contrasts against all the gentle sucking and licking that's going on elsewhere.

That oiled finger circles, and Cal's teeth nip at my nipple again.

The first orgasm clouds my mind like frost on a windowpane.

If I had any lingering doubts that these men were right for me, that orgasm erases it. They work my body like they're members of an orchestra and I'm the strings they're plucking. Fuck.

Gus chuckles when he feels me start to shake, then he plunges his tongue into my mouth, deepening our kiss and intensifying everything. Bryn sucks hard at my neck, and all five of them work to draw the pleasurable sensations out as long as they possibly can.

When my tense muscles finally relax, I'm not given a second of reprieve.

"I want to taste our cookie first," Dem announces.

"No fair. You were already down there, and I might fall asleep if I have to wait," Bryn argues. "I should get to lick her." Gus breaks off our kiss when Bryn stands, jostling me a bit as his mouth leaves my neck. The sloth demon stomps around the side of my little kitchen island and shoves Dem. The two of them get into a wrestling match over tongue-fucking me.

Part of me loves that brutish battle for dominance and wants to sit up and watch, but the other three won't let me. Before I know it, Cal's climbing up onto the countertop, his naked form a sight to behold. I didn't realize he had such a defined six-pack. He straddles my chest, and my eyes move from his stomach down to the huge cock that juts towards my face. His dick is maybe six inches long, but it makes up in girth what it lacks in length. I lift my hand to touch his dick, wondering if I can even get my fingers closed around it. The answer is barely.

Cal shoves up his glasses and then meets my eyes, a domineering look crossing his features. "Shove your tits together, Joy."

There is something so hot about a guy who wants to use every part of me. I shove my hand on either side of my breasts and press them together. They aren't huge, and there's no way his massive dick will…

His dick prods at the entrance to my mouth. "Lube me up," he orders. My mouth slides open, but my eyes search for Gus, wondering if he's mad that Cal's basically taking me over.

But Gus is watching us, his eyes dark as his hand slides steadily up and down his dick. His piercing glints in the light, and once again, I find myself wondering what it will feel like when he finally fucks me.

When.

Definitely when.

I start taking as much of Cal's thick dick in my mouth as I can while Nico slides his fingers around my over sensitized clit, making me twist my hips to try to get away. "Oh no, lass, I warned you. I'm not leaving this spot until I've seen you come at least five times."

I want to curse at him, but my mouth is currently occupied. I can't get more than a few inches before my cheeks are stretched to their maximum capacity.

Cal doesn't press though. He simply pulls back and says, "If you can't fit it, you'll have to figure out some other way to lube it up."

Gus clears his throat, and when I turn to look at him, at first, I think his gaze is burning with jealousy. But when his eyes flicker to Cal's cock and then back to me, I realize it's intensity, not jealousy. These demons are probably used to wild orgies. Everyone fucking everyone.

The mental image that accompanies that thought makes my pussy flutter, on the edge of a second spasm.

"Gus," I ask slowly, carefully measuring his reaction to each word, "will you lick Cal's cock with me?"

Gus nods, his eyes lit up with a dark excitement. I lean up a little further as Gus comes closer. I position my head on one side of Cal's thick dick, while Gus leans close to me. Together, we extend our tongues and lap at the underside of Cal's dick, our tongues meeting and shoving at one another.

Above us, Cal moans, but my eyes are locked on Gus. I'm completely enraptured by the fact that he's willing to do what I asked. Part of me wants to know if he'll go further.

I lean back just long enough to order, "Gus, play with my nipples and his balls at the same time."

My wrath demon doesn't hesitate. He continues to lave Cal's thick, veiny cock while one hand reaches out and tweaks my nipple. His other goes up to fondle Cal's thick balls. I return my tongue to battling his, and soon, our entire mouths are involved, sucking either side of Cal's cock while we attempt to kiss around it.

It's the hottest thing I've ever done, made even hotter by the fact that my wrath demon will do anything to please me. With one more twist of my nipple, Gus sets me off, and Nico growls his excitement as I come.

"I can see your pussy clenching," Nico declares.

"Fucking hell, man, that was supposed to be my orgasm," Bryn complains, because apparently, he and Dem have stopped fighting to watch.

"Dammit," Dem says. "Fine. Go."

I hear their chatter as background noise, barely a buzz against my ears, because Gus has suddenly grabbed my hair and pulled me off of Cal's dick so he can plunge his tongue into my mouth. He tastes of Cal's pre-cum, which is so fucking hot.

Cal shoves his lubed-up dick between my breasts and helps me push them together further as he thrusts, the tip of his dick emerging with each stroke. It only takes a few before my chin and Gus's are splattered with hot cum. We don't stop making out, because somehow, this nasty little endeavor has tied me to Gus in a deeper way than I've ever experienced before.

I grab the back of Gus's dark hair and pull him in closer as Cal climbs off. Then I shove him away and say, "You're next. Climb up so you can fuck my mouth."

"My body's yours, my queen, just like my mind and my heart and the wisp that is my soul," he responds.

I'm momentarily stunned into silence. But as he moves to obey me, Bryn starts to lick around my pussy lips, and any questions I have about Gus's random poetic outburst fade. After coming twice without fingers or dick inside of me, I'm desperate to move beyond foreplay. I'm desperate to clench around something, anything, even his tongue. I reach down and shove his face squarely on my slit.

"Lick me," I beg. I can't stand to be teased more, not when Nico's already drawing figure eights on my clit and smiling every time he sees my hips twist, that fucker. He's going to get some serious edging when his turn comes, I decide.

Bryn, however, is nothing like naughty Nico. He just aims to please. Or maybe aims to finish as soon as he can, so we can move on to post-sex sleepy cuddles. His tongue starts lapping up my cum with a contented sigh. "So good," he mumbles against my pussy lips. Yes. His tongue is so good. So tantalizing. I start to float off the countertop, my hips rising, my thighs almost ready to clench his head in a death grip.

Nico's finger slides down from my clit just before I can come a third time. "Dammit, frustration demon," I growl.

He just laughs and slowly slides his finger back, touching too lightly and slowly for me to reach that peak again.

Meanwhile, Gus looms over me, his body a tattooed masterpiece. His barbell runs vertically through his glans, the tip of his dick. I'm so entranced by the sight of it and the smear of pre-cum on the head of his penis that I lean forward and immediately open my mouth. Once he's in past my teeth, I realize my demon is one smart fucker. I'm not going to pop his dick out of my mouth and risk banging my teeth on a regular basis, so he's going to get deepthroat treatment.

He can tell the moment I realize this, because my eyes fly up to meet his and one of those rare smiles lights his face. I slide him deeper in my throat in response, letting the metal of his piercing slide along my tongue and slowly into my throat.

He groans when I force myself to swallow hard, clenching around him. I can only hold him in that position for a few seconds before I have to release and open my mouth. He pulls back and stares down at me. "Want me to wait and take your ass?"

I nearly growl at him, but then Bryn's tongue slides deep inside me, stroking me just right, and Nico decides to stop fucking around as my eyes drift shut in pleasure. He pinches my clit and pulls. A string of Christmas lights blink on behind my eyelids, bright blotches of color and happiness wrap around me until...I scream as I spread Christmas cheer all over Bryn's face.

Gus gives me a minute to recover before he grabs my hand, licks up my palm, and then shoves it on top of his dick. "Stroke and suck," he orders, turning the tables on me. I happily comply.

I hear Dem's voice say, "My turn." And suddenly, new hands are on my hips, palms and fingertips that are rougher than Bryn's. Heated flesh teases my opening, and I realize that it's the tip of Dem's dick.

Was I intimidated about multiple guys before? That was pre-three orgasms. Now I mumble around Gus's dick, "Put it in me."

Seconds later, my pussy and mouth are both stretched wide as two of my demons take me. I've never been this blissed out. It's better than meditation.

They build up a rhythm and both gradually work their way deeper, and I want to cry because I'm literally so happy and overwhelmed. Then it hits me. These demons stayed. They've kept their word. They've helped rebuild Christmas Village and Santa's Workshop. And they aren't going anywhere. They're mine, and I'm theirs.

I come with a wail that vibrates Gus's cock, and Dem digs into my hips, tossing one of my feet up over his shoulder so that he can stroke me nice and deep.

He grunts as he fucks me hard, and if I could reach him, I'd yank his hair as hard as I could. He changes his angle, thrusting up a bit and slamming into my G-spot a couple times before he moans. As soon as I feel his hot jets of cum shoot inside of me, I release Gus from my mouth. My throat rasps, sore from the press of his piercing, but the longing inside of me remains intense. "Fuck me."

Gus slides off the countertop, and I stare at Nico with hooded eyes as the huge redheaded fucker keeps thumbing my poor clit.

"You're gonna bruise her."

"No, I'm gonna toughen her up. She's going to learn to love it," he responds, tweaking my sensitive nub and making the nerve endings in my thighs sputter.

"When's your turn?" I ask him as Gus lines up.

"Soon enough, lass. You've got one more to go by my count," he tells me before he glances over at Gus. "Give it to her good."

My wrath demon's eyes light on mine as he slowly slides in, and that delicious barbell drags along my insides. He stares down at me. "Can I use my power on you?" he moans as he seats himself all the way to the root.

"Power?" I ask, half lost in sensation.

"Say yes," Nico urges. "Angry sex is hot."

My eyes widen, and I glance up at Gus. "Just a little," I whisper. His hands cup my thighs, and he releases his magic in tiny bursts. My body temperature rises and my vision narrows as fury surges through me like a tidal wave.

I reach up and latch onto Gus's shoulders, my nails digging into his flesh. I've felt angry before, yes, but as a half-angel, that fury has always been a muted feeling. Now, combined with the drag of that amazing dick and the flick of Nico's fingers, it's a wildfire. Emotions burn through me, and I grow feral, thrusting my hips up wildly and ruining Gus's tempo until he speeds up.

Nico starts to whisper dirty things in my ear. "Yeah, you ken I like to watch you fook him. You look classy, but underneath, you're dirty. You bonnie little angel. My dirty girl. You love me staring at your fannie, don't you, Joy? Admit it. You like knowing that dick inside of you is from Hell, yeah? You like being a bad girl. Our bad girl."

"Yes, yes, yes," I chant. But soon, I'm incapable of speech. I'm incapable of doing anything more than licking the salty bead of sweat from Gus's shoulder before biting him, hard. That spurs him on, and he fucks faster, the sound of our bodies smashing together filling the cabin, and I scream as Nico and Gus take me to that peak for a fifth time.

I collapse back onto the countertop, utterly spent, and mutter, "Merry Christmas to me."

Nico chuckles. "Oh, Christmas is just getting started, little mate. We're gonna give you a bath, and then we'll have round two of presents."

I shake my head weakly. "No. No more presents."

He leans down and whispers in my ear, "A girl can never have too many presents." And you know what? He sweeps me up and carries me off to my clawfoot tub. And after Nico has gently washed all the cum from my body, he uses his mouth, his hands, and his dick to prove that's true.

EPILOGUE

JOY

I PLACE my hand on my rounded stomach, my smile broadening when the babe immediately begins to kick at my palm. Not even born yet, and already, she's taking after her daddies.

Her daddies, who are currently attempting to tie the sack of toys to the top of the sleigh.

"Be careful!" I bring my mug of steaming hot chocolate to my lips, steam wafting from the marshmallowy top, and take a long sip, the warmth of the drink soothing my very soul and defrosting my frigid fingers. It's a surprisingly tranquil day, the blankets of compacted snow glistening like thousands of diamonds in the midday sun. The wind is practically non-existent, only the tiniest of breezes stirring my blonde hair.

"I'm always careful," Cal retorts immediately as he balances at the top of the magical sleigh, his feet precariously close to the edge. Nico smirks at the white lie demon before he throws him the sack of toys—magically enchanted to remain only a few feet tall despite housing all of the presents for every child in the human world.

"Yer such a fookin liar," Nico exclaims cheerfully as Cal positions the bag in the back of the white sleigh accented in gold.

I take a moment to admire both demons. Cal's currently wearing a red, pressed suit, one that conforms to his naturally muscular build. His sandy-blond hair is longer than it has ever been before, coming to rest near his ears. He still wears his customary glasses, though this particular pair has red and green rims.

Nico, on the other hand, is bedecked in a Christmas tree kilt and an ugly Christmas sweater, mainly because he knows the outfit irritates both Gus and my father. The sweater has a reindeer nose directly in the center of his stomach, and when he presses it, it glows a bright cherry red. The back of the sweater has a rein-deer tail sticking out of a rather realistic looking deer butt. It's honestly atrocious…but the outfit only makes me love him more.

"They'll be fine." I'd recognize Dem's sultry voice anywhere, and a moment later, my back is pressed against his front, the hard line of his cock poking against my ass through the material of his jeans. His hands move around my waist to settle on my stomach. On cue, the baby begins to kick. "She's taken after her mother," he muses, and I can hear the amusement lacing his voice.

"Funny. I was just thinking the same thing in reverse— that she's like all of you." I use both hands to bring my hot chocolate back to my lips, but before the rim of the cup can make contact, the drink is stolen from my hands. "Hey!" I exclaim in a half-hearted protest as Dem dances around me, drinking my coco. He merely sticks his tongue out at me, his eyes alight with impish joy.

"Don't tip the bag over!" my dad bellows, and a moment later, the big man himself steps out from the tree line where he was lurking—read as, stalking—his eyebrows pinched together and his frown forlorn. Dad made the tough decision to retire last year, and though he planned for me to take over...

Things changed, if my very pregnant belly is any indication.

"I got it," Cal lies as the bag begins to topple over the side of the sleigh, very nearly hitting Vixen in the nose. The female reindeer makes a face, nose scrunching, before her expression turns almost…sultry. Seductive. If that's even possible for a reindeer. Dad swears to me that Vixen and the rest of the herd are all normal reindeer, but apparently, the little minx has developed a crush on my demons, probably from the time the cherubs attempted to mate them so many years ago. I kinda want to be jealous, but again, she's a *fucking* reindeer.

The bag of toys lands on the grass beside the sleigh, and I swear I hear the sound of glass shattering. If Cal broke any of the toys the day before Christmas…

Gus materializes seemingly out of thin air and rips the bag open, sticking his entire head inside. He straightens once more, his customary scowl still firmly in place. "Nothing's broken."

Gus, like Cal, is wearing a suit as well, only his is as white as mountaintop snow with red sleeves and a matching red tie. He also wears a Santa hat that jingles when he walks.

"For heaven's sake…" Dad pinches the bridge of his nose, attempting to do some of those deep breathing exercises his yoga instructor has taught him, when Bryn's head pops up over the side of the sleigh. How long has he been sleeping in there?

I smile indulgently at my husband, who blinks rapidly, running his fingers through his shaggy brown hair.

"Where...where am I?" He yawns, throwing his arms up above his head and causing his shirt to ride up, revealing a sliver of bronze skin. Instantly, my panties turn damp when I think about all of the sacrilegious things I want to do to that particular swath of skin. Taste it. Lick it. Nip it. Fuck—

"Soon, beautiful," Dem whispers in my ear, one of his hands coming to rest on my shoulder while he continues to hold my hot chocolate with his other one.

"You don't even know what I'm thinking," I fire back, though at this point in our marriage, he probably does. They all do, if the suggestive looks they throw me behind Santa's back are any indication. If only Cal and Gus didn't have to travel around the world tonight...

At least I have three other demons to keep me company while Cal and Gus play Santa.

"Did you do a reindeer check?" Dad shoots off, turning to stare intently at the reindeer already hooked to the sleigh. Gus's scowl deepens.

"Of course."

"We didn't," Cal says at the same time, and we all roll our eyes. Fucking white lie demons.

"Feed them their carrots?" Santa presses.

"And cookies!" Nico throws in helpfully, flashing a wink my way. "Reindeer always perform better with cookies."

"And did you oil the sleigh?" Dad lifts a white eyebrow, and this time, I step forward, coming to stand beside my father and placing a hand on his shoulder comfortingly. His eyes soften when he sees me, and he immediately adopts a baby voice when he focuses on my stomach. "How's my favorite grandbaby doing? Are you being a good girl for your mommy? Grandpa loves you so much."

Because apparently, babies make even the most feared and dangerous archangels into coddling fools.

"Dad, they have this," I promise him, turning to spear each of my guys with a long, loving look. Over the past few years, they have quickly become my entire world. I love them with an intensity that leaves me breathless, even after all of this time, and I know they feel the same. They care about Christmas just as much as I do, if only *because* I do. They want the happiest, jolliest world possible for our little baby, and I know that they won't screw this up.

Dad still seems unsure, the lines between his eyes deepening, but after a moment, he nods, albeit begrudgingly.

"You need to trust your son-in-laws," I press as his eyes lift from my belly to my face.

"All right. I suppose I need to stop…helicoptering." He makes another face at the term my demons taught him as Cal and Gus move to join me, one on either side.

"We'll make this the best Christmas ever," Gus promises.

"Well, maybe the second-best Christmas ever," Cal amends, the lying fucktard. Both men immediately pull me in between them, their hands resting on my belly and caressing it through the fabric of my red gown.

"This is our home," Nico adds as he moves to stand beside Gus.

"And Joy and this baby are our lives," adds Bryn around a yawn. He stands on the other side of Cal.

"And trust me." Dem moves forward to join my line of men. All of them beautiful. All of them handsome. All of them kind and witty and sarcastic and perfect. And all of them mine, now and forever. "With us in charge, this will be one Christmas that no one will ever forget."

Want more demons? Check out the Darkest Flames series set in the same universe!

ACKNOWLEDGMENTS

Special thanks to all of the people who helped us get this book together.

Thank you to Bookish Dreams Editing for helping us polish this brimstone.

And thank you Carol Marques Designs for the beautiful cover.

ABOUT THE AUTHORS

Ann and Katie are very dedicated to research, so they went to heaven and hell during the course of this book, sat on Santa's lap, ate lots of Christmas cookies, and petted some very fine-looking reindeer, who unfortunately were not possessed by hot demons. Thanks for reading!

ALSO BY KATIE MAY

Beyond the Shadows

(Horror Reverse Harem, COMPLETED)

Book 1

Gangs and Ghosts

Book 2

Guns and Graveyards

Book 3

Gallows and Ghouls

The Damning

(Fantasy Paranormal Reverse Harem)

Book 1

Greed

Book 2

Envy

Book 3

Gluttony

Prodigium Academy
(Horror Comedy Academy Reverse Harem)

Book 1
Monsters

Book 2
Roaring

Tory's School for the Trouble
(Bully Horror Academy Reverse Harem)

Book 1
Between

Book 2
Untitled (Coming Summer 2020)

Supernaturalette
(Interactive Reverse Harem)

Book 1
Introductions

Book 2

First Dates

Book 3

Group Outing

CO-WRITES

Afterworld Academy with Loxley Savage

(Academy Fantasy Reverse Harem)

Book 1

Dearly Departed

Book 2

Darkness Deceives

Her Immortal Legacy with Elena Lawson

(Time Travel Paranormal Reverse Harem)

Book 1

Chasing Time

Book 2

Finding Time (Coming Soon)

Darkest Flames with Ann Denton
(Paranormal Reverse Harem)

Book 1
Demon Kissed

Book 1.5
Demon Stalked

Book 2
Demon Loved (Coming Soon)

STAND-ALONES

Toxicity
(Contemporary Reverse Harem)

Blindly Indicted
(Prison Reverse Harem)

Not All Heroes Wear Capes (Just Dresses)
(Short Comedic Reverse Harem)

Charming Devils
(Bully/Revenge Reverse Harem)

Goddess of Pain

A medium-burn paranormal heist reverse harem with a badass main character.

Magical Academy for Delinquents #MAD - Book 1

Delinquents Turned Fugitives #DTF - Book 2

MAGE SHIFTER WAR SERIES
(Duet Complete)

A medium-burn paranormal mafia reverse harem with shifters and fae. Kidnapping and enemy themes. Co-written with Elle Middaugh.

Fae Captive - Book 1

Fae Unchained - Book 2

HAMMER TIME
(Standalone)

A medium-burn paranormal comedy reverse harem featuring lots of ancient deities and potty humor. Co-written with MJ Marstens.

Lotto Love Series
(Completed Duet)

A medium-burn, contemporary, romantic comedy reverse harem about winning the lotto and doing whatever the hell you want with it.

Lotto Men - Book 1

Lotto Trouble - Book 2

Ruby - Jewels Cafe Series
(Standalone)

A fated mates medium burn reverse harem with angels, demons, and Christmas miracles.

The Lyon Fox Mysteries

An urban fantasy / cozy mystery series with a magicless fae, a lot of laughs, and a dash of romance.

Magical Murder - Book 1

Enchanted Execution - Book 2

Supernatural Sleep - Book 3

Hexed Hit - Book 4

TIMEBEND SERIES

A post-apocalyptic fantasy thriller series.

Melt - Book 1

Burn - Book 2